THE ROAD BETWEEN US

ALSO BY BINDU SURESH

26 Knots

THE ROAD BETWEEN US

BINDU SURESH

Assembly Press
PRINCE EDWARD COUNTY, ONTARIO

Library and Archives Canada Cataloguing in Publication

Title: The road between us / Bindu Suresh.
Names: Suresh, Bindu, 1983- author
Identifiers: Canadiana (print) 20250133202 | Canadiana (ebook) 20250133474 | ISBN 9781998336173 (softcover) | ISBN 9781998336180 (EPUB)
Subjects: LCGFT: Novels.
Classification: LCC PS8637.U754 R63 2025 | DDC C813/.6—dc23

Published by Assembly Press | assemblypress.ca
Cover and interior designed by Greg Tabor
Edited by Leigh Nash

Printed and bound in Canada on uncoated paper made from 100% recycled content in line with our commitment to ethical business practices and sustainability.

for my cousin, Varun Kowsik

ESTELA

Estela's mouth was dry as she dialed the familiar number. She remembered his tentative big toe caressing her calf as they lay next to each other, her jerk away from him, the uncomfortable night spent huddled at the edge of his double bed. The next morning—almost fourteen years ago now—she'd finished her stovetop coffee and left his New York apartment, stealing away while he was still in the shower.

"Ash?" she said, when he answered.

He paused. "Estela?" he asked, slowly.

"A blast from the past, right?"

Estela had heard only bits and pieces about Ash's life in the years since they'd last spoken. From a colleague at her law firm whose husband also worked in the foreign service, she learned Ash had gotten promoted and moved to Beijing. A friend of a friend had tagged him in a social media post in Brazil: cocktail in hand, dark sunglasses concealing his eyes, bearded. And, in an email exchange Estela had initiated just a few months ago—with superficial details about where she lived now and the new guy she was seeing—Ash shared how he'd gotten home from a boys' weekend in Tremblant, one-carat engagement ring in his pocket, to a cold, darkened house, his girlfriend's goodbye note on their front-entrance table. *I thought all weekend about how I wanted a life with her just as she was thinking she wanted to leave*, he'd written.

On the other end of the line, Ash was silent.

Estela continued. "This is going to be superawkward, but I need your help."

They'd met at McGill, in line for student cards. Estela had been waiting behind him for a few minutes before he turned around.

"Are you a first-year, too?"

Estela nodded. Ash was wearing a blue backpack with a paper-airplane motif on the shoulder straps. His thick-framed, square glasses amplified his dark eyelashes. It was sunny and still warm enough that they were both wearing shorts. They were near the end of the line, next to a bed of yellow marigolds.

"What are you taking?" he asked.

"English, I think," Estela said.

"History and poli-sci," he said, placing his hand on his chest as if swearing an oath. "What do you want to be when you grow up?"

"An English prof, maybe?" she said. "You?"

"Yeah, maybe a history prof. Or maybe a diplomat?"

They covered the usual ground: he had an apartment with three high school friends on Jeanne-Mance; she had lucked out and gotten a single dorm room in Douglas. Ash was from Calgary; Estela was from Ottawa. Both had come to Montreal to get away from home.

"It's not even that I don't like home," Ash said as they neared the front of the line. "And I know all teenagers must think this, but I feel like I've been ready to be on my own for a while now. And moving out here was the only way to make sure that happened."

His parents, both doctors, had offered him the penthouse of a new condo near the University of Calgary if he stayed. He'd asked if he could go to Europe for the summer with the money they'd save if he didn't. They said no.

"Which I guess is fair enough," he said, laughing.

Ash and Estela exchanged phone numbers, but before either had a chance to send the other a message, they ran into each other in the middle of campus on the first day of class.

"Hey!" Ash said, walking out of the Arts Building. Estela was leaning against one of the pillars that made up the stone facade.

"Hi," Estela replied. "What's up?"

"I just got out of class. The History of Modern Europe. Also known as All the History You Already Learned in High School. Want to have lunch?"

"I have class."

"Can I come?"

"Really?" she asked. "Don't you want to know what class it is?"

"Not really," Ash said, smiling.

They walked the short distance to Leacock and entered the main auditorium, Estela placing her satchel on the seat to her right as Ash took the seat to her left. Five minutes into the professor's introductory remarks, Ash leaned over and whispered, "I haven't read any Mordecai Richler. Does that make me a bad Canadian?" He dutifully took notes. And halfway through the lecture, when he moved his knee an inch to the right to rest against hers, Estela didn't pull away.

The brush of his knee might have turned into holding hands while walking through the Roddick Gates, into looking through graduate course catalogues together, into joint leases and a marriage proposal that was accepted, not unspoken and unheard—except that at a house party, one in fact thrown by Ash to cement his flirtation with Estela, Estela met Langston.

The night of the party, Estela stepped over the tangle of shoes in the entranceway, a six-pack of depanneur beer in hand, the girl she'd befriended from the dorm room across from hers following close behind. She found Ash slicing limes in the kitchen.

"Hey!" he said, kissing her cheek.

"Hey," she said. "This is Clara," she continued, with a nod toward the girl behind her.

"Cool." He shook Clara's hand.

Later that night, on seeing Estela, her back against the trellis in the garden, her right hand in Langston's left, his other palm against her cheek, and his lips—though Ash couldn't see clearly in the early dusk and weak lamplight—almost certainly against her neck, Ash reached for a woman's hand as she walked by, a woman who happened to be Clara.

Estela and Langston dated for two months. Ash and Clara dated for two years, and in the year and ten months that Estela was single, each time she ran into Ash at the dorm elevators she felt the tug in her chest, the stone falling from her throat into the pit of her stomach, that he was there to see Clara and not her.

Estela knocked on Professor Arshovsky's door. It was the fall of her third year. She heard the shuffle of a stack of papers, then his footfalls. After a brief pause, the door opened.

"Sorry about that," he said. "Estela, right? I suppose I should leave my door open when I claim to be having office hours."

He invited her in. He motioned to a straight-backed antique chair across from his desk and asked her to sit.

"I got your email. You're in my Milton class and had a question about Chaos in *Paradise Lost*, correct? With a view to this being your topic for your mid-term paper?"

"Yes, exactly." She took a hesitant step over the threshold.

"You're an English major?" he asked.

"Yes. I'm in my third year."

"How do you like the class so far?"

"I like it. I love the reading list," Estela said. "The class is so big it's hard to get a question in, though."

"Well, that's what these office hours are for." He laughed. "Please, sit. And call me Roman."

Soon Estela was seeing Roman weekly. She confessed that her favourite book, before she'd discovered *Mrs. Dalloway*, had been *Interview with the Vampire*. He told her about his recent divorce and how hard he'd fought for fifty-fifty custody. She told him about the night she'd hidden under the piano, in the half-dark of the half-moon, listening to her father sob in the kitchen, his weeping muffled by her mother's shoulder, when he'd learned of his mother's death. For her birthday, at the end of September, Roman gave Estela his copy of *Utopia*, printed in 1751, the one he'd found at a used book sale during his undergraduate years at the University of Toronto.

So when Estela, half sitting against the side of his desk, nervous and unable to meet his eyes, asked him for a letter of reference for graduate school, Roman said yes.

And when he came to sit next to her and placed his hand on her leg, Estela let him.

What happened next, she let happen, too.

The following day—an unseasonably warm one in early October—Estela went to the student health centre for emergency contraception. The waiting room was airless and humid; the girl sitting next to her tore a single sheet of paper from a coiled notebook and fashioned it into a fan. An electronic display read *Now Serving C16*. Estela held C25. In the forty minutes she'd been waiting, only one patient had been called in.

When it became evident she wouldn't see the nurse before noon, she texted Ash to cancel their lunch plans: *Hey, I'm not going to make it, something came up!* Ash immediately responded: *Sure. Everything okay?* A few seconds later, while still deciding how to reply to Ash, she got a message from Roman: *I hope you're feeling okay about yesterday. Would love to take you out for dinner tonight if you're free.*

Estela flipped her phone closed.

She replied to both texts from home later that afternoon—after she'd finally been seen by the nurse and given a pill to swallow, along with a second dose in a sealed white envelope, to be taken twelve hours later—claiming illness, hours spent vomiting, a lie that, soon afterwards, came true.

Estela did have dinner with Roman, a few days later, in Villeray. They fell back into the comfortable routine they'd had before: meeting platonically at cafés during the week and speaking on the phone, often. Once, on a Wednesday, they went to a hotel, but it felt so impersonal—it felt so clear that they were hiding—that the next time Roman suggested it, Estela declined.

Estela and Roman made love in his office, mostly in the mornings on weekends, when the rest of Montreal was still asleep but the two of them were searingly, blindingly awake. They used his desk, cleared of graduate students' papers and the notes for his own research, or the straight-backed chair, Roman sitting upright, she in his lap, her ankles on his shoulders and his fingers spread, grasping her hips. They avoided any other place: hers was out as she had three roommates, one of whom was in one of his introductory lectures; as was his, with his ex-wife's unexpected visits with their young son.

Estela denied being in love with him, the one time Ash asked.

"It's just that you're not dating anyone else," he'd said.

"It's not like he's breaking the law," Estela said. "We're both fully consenting adults."

"That wasn't the point of my question at all," Ash replied.

She thought back to that first day at his office with shame. Shame that she hadn't seen it coming—that she'd had no idea that he would place his hand on her leg and then slowly move it higher, she shifting slightly to accommodate his rise up her inner thigh. Shame that she hadn't had a Brazilian in months, and that when she'd finally shown herself to him, naked, she had been ungroomed, unsightly.

A month after her initial visit, Estela went back to the clinic. She explained to the intake nurse that her period was late despite the morning-after pills. She was given a cup to pee in, then told to sit and wait.

Estela was reading an ad for translation services—the kind with a dozen or so tearable strips at the bottom—when her ticket number appeared on the display. She followed the nurse's aide down the hall and into an examination room. A Frida Kahlo print hung on the wall; Estela stared at the portrait's grotesque anatomic hearts as she sat on the exam table and slid her feet into the stirrups.

With the gestational age confirmed, the nurse asked Estela to book her procedure for no later than the coming week. The receptionist let her pick the date, so she chose the twelfth of November.

It was already the worst day of Estela's life; at least this way she wouldn't ruin another one.

Most years, Estela spent the anniversary of her brother's death on a park bench, her fingers and toes going numb from the cold as she sat for hours, willing herself to remember him: how they'd steal popsicles out of the freezer in the nurses' lounge as they waited for their mother's shift to end, giggling behind one of the sofas, their hands sticky with melted strawberry juice; how he'd loved the rainbow streamers affixed to the handlebars of his hand-me-down bicycle, the pink BMX that had originally been hers. Their pre-bedtime Nintendo marathons, with her as Mario and him as Luigi, his console tossed to the side and his head buried under a cushion when it came time to fight the final boss. More recently, unable to recall Ethan's features without a cue, she'd pull out the photo she carried in her wallet.

One November, convinced that her commemoration had become candy-coated and therefore false, that she was losing the truth of him, Estela focused on their fights: the Boxing Day he'd raided the chocolate box gifted to their father by his department's secretary and had eaten three out of the four chocolate-covered Brazil nuts, when they'd always shared them two and two, or the birthday he'd hidden her new juggling set in his room and said nothing as she'd searched frantically to find it.

But how detailed those memories were—the resting expression of his face, which she'd forgotten, the layout of the upstairs rooms that comprised their little world, Ethan's beloved race car bed frame—left a tight, frayed knot in her stomach, one that wouldn't loosen even when she unclenched her fists and drew in long, measured breaths.

On the November 12 of her first year of university, she left all of her dirty dishes in Langston's small sink and her pyjamas on the bathroom floor, and lay on his bed with her laptop on her stomach, watching movies all day. Langston asked what was wrong, and when she answered that she couldn't tell him, the weight that settled into his eyes added another layer to her grief, like a second slab of snow coming to rest over a man buried in an avalanche.

On November 12 of her third year, Estela missed her parents' usual call on the anniversary of Ethan's death for the first time. She'd been on a ketamine drip—as he'd put her under, the doctor had said, *Think of a pleasant beach*, and she'd thought of their family vacation in Guadeloupe when Ethan was three, of running after him down to the water's edge, afraid he'd be taken by the waves—and had been too woozy later to return their call.

Ash had picked her up after her appointment. She'd told him she was getting an IUD put in—which wasn't entirely untrue, as they'd done so immediately after the abortion.

Estela had been pregnant for six weeks—not long enough for the embryo to have been visibly male or female, even under the most high-powered of microscopes—and already she'd been certain it would have been a boy, and that she would have named him Ethan Patrick, after her brother and her paternal grandmother, Patricia.

Between her second clinic visit and the date of her abortion, Estela couldn't bear to see Roman. She dodged his cheerful texts with excuse after excuse, finally placating him when she agreed to a weekend getaway in Orford at the end of November.

On the car ride there, he described the trips he'd taken to the Eastern Townships with his mother, the daylong hikes they'd done together while his father stayed home with Roman's grandfather, who had kidney failure.

"We didn't ever talk about it this way, but it was a nice break for the two of us." He opened his window briefly to defog the windshield. "From the weight of it. My dad's dad, this intrepid, plucky Eastern European immigrant, permanently bedridden and on dialysis."

They drove through Brossard, then past Saint-Jean-sur-Richelieu, then Granby. Through the window, Estela noticed a copse of trees, alone in a field of yellow. The secret she kept was lodged between them, a tiny, irritating seed, a pea under her seat cushion, a secret that had weighed a gram but felt like a ton. Roman felt like a stranger to her now; Estela drew her knees together and shifted them to the right, toward the passenger door.

Roman went on. "We had an old trail guide from the fifties, and we'd pick a new hike from it every Saturday. We were on a particularly long one when we heard the news, maybe halfway through, that my grandfather had died. The park warden trekked five kilometres uphill to tell us."

Roman flicked on the turn signal and overtook a small red car with two brown leather suitcases and a bicycle, lying on its side, roped to the roof.

"I was sad, of course. My grandfather had been a huge part of my life, especially when I was younger, before he got sick. But I remember looking ahead at the wide trail, at the overhanging trees, and wishing that we could keep going. I was disappointed we had to turn back."

The autumn sun, low in the sky, turned the clouds and hayfields on either side of the highway purple.

"I still feel terrible about that," he said.

They drove in silence for a few minutes.

"Anyway," Roman said, glancing at Estela, finally realizing that she was looking out the window, not at him, "I'm excited to take you. I'm excited for you to see more of Quebec than just Montreal."

When they made love that night, it was like a fight. Estela stared at the ceiling, refusing to meet Roman's eyes. He, in turn, focused on the pillow beside her cheek, pounding into her harder the more she looked away. When he at last collapsed, exhausted, beside her, Estela struggled to fall asleep. She thought about her last interaction with Ash—she'd barely spoken to him, either, over the last few weeks—when he'd picked her up from the clinic. She didn't remember much from that drive home, only that Ash had said, *Promise me you'll tell me what this was really about, one day*, and that, paused at an intersection, he'd held her hand.

That night, over the course of unrelated dreams, and her waking, disoriented, between them, Estela forgave Roman. How, after all, to blame him for a consequence she'd never even mentioned, to blame him when she'd never even given him the chance to act well?

When she awoke, his left leg was draped over her, and she felt lighter despite its weight. As if the distance between them had been shortened, a chasm bridged, overnight—leaving just the inch or two between his lips and the nape of her neck, the warmth of his breath on her skin.

What Estela didn't ask herself: why not tell Roman, if not for the fear that he would in turn blame her, wonder out loud why she'd said nothing about not being on the pill, why she hadn't stopped and asked him to wear a condom?

Why, if not for the fear that she, in fact, were to blame?

A year into Estela's master's degree in comparative literature at the University of Toronto, her supervisor emailed to suggest they meet immediately after their Friday translation seminar. Estela had submitted her thesis outline the night before; the check-in probably meant it had been obvious she'd thrown together her list of intended references at the last minute, half-drunk.

She'd started writing a few days before the deadline, quite sober—until she realized that her lower-year coursework in Milton had informed her fourth-year seminar choice, which had then suggested a particular focus for her master's thesis, which she was now stuck with as it had been the grounds for her admission, and which would require her to cite, at length, two of Roman's articles, as well as his book, which were seminal works in their field. Estela had then completed her proposal with a beer, followed by another two, and then the half-finished bottle of wine she'd found at the back of her fridge.

Over the course of the evening, she kept returning to McGill's Department of English website to look through the faculty profiles—ostensibly to correctly spell the names of the professors whose lectures she'd attended, for her references list—her cursor repeatedly coming to rest beside Roman's handsome face.

"It just isn't clear to me that you really want this," Professor Matani said to Estela during their meeting. The professor paced during her lectures and did so as well here, in her office, the plush carpet worn where she now trod, in front of the window. It was a grey, cloudy September day, and a light rain percussed the gridded windows.

"One of the most useful things I was told early in my English degree is that academia isn't simply a continuation of your undergraduate coursework. The focus shifts from learning to producing. From primary sources to secondary sources. You have to really love research. That's your job. Not learning. Not teaching."

Estela studied the objects on her supervisor's desk: a letter opener shaped like half a pair of scissors, a series of Post-it Notes of different colours arranged in a vertical line beside her laptop, a photo with her husband and son at a waterfall, turned at an angle and only half-visible to the person seated across from her desk. Framed on the walls, her diplomas: one from Princeton, the other from Stanford. And that same red, leather-bound Shakespeare—the same edition Roman had—displayed on a large wooden bookshelf.

"I wanted to have this talk early because I want you to think about whether you truly want to be here. Whether you're here for the right reasons."

Estela wondered, at that second, if Professor Matani knew, somehow, about her affair with Roman.

"We love you here. Obviously. You're smart. You're a smart woman with original ideas and I would love to see you succeed," she continued. "But not at your own expense."

Back at her studio apartment, Estela confronted the truth she'd avoided since things had ended with Roman: that the career path she'd chosen was inextricable from him. The best place for her PhD was back at McGill; given their allied interests, she could have no more suited an advisor than Roman himself. Even if Estela kept her vow to never set foot on the McGill campus again, she and Roman would forever be colleagues, contemporaries, collaborators. They would see each other at conferences. They would comment on each other's work. And for many years, given his head start, Roman would be, in all of this, her superior.

Estela sat at her desk and opened her laptop. Her browser was still open to the McGill Department of English website. Outside her window, a funnel of steam escaped from a building vent across the street.

She highlighted the address bar, typed *University of Ottawa law school*, and hit Enter.

It was the first warm spring day in April. Estela's father was outside securing the last box of odds and ends into the U-Haul. Estela surveyed her empty apartment as if she could still see the furniture there, like phantom limbs: her desk, and the wall it sat against whose every notch and scratch she'd memorized; the table in the kitchen area where she'd sat with Giselle, laughing, going through boxes of necklaces and handbags for their trunk shows; and the bed, the double bed from IKEA that required two people to assemble—two lovers, two best friends, two roommates—when she'd just moved to Toronto and had no one, not a single friend, not Ash, not Roman. The bed she'd finally constructed alone by lifting the side rail with her big toe and tightening the screw in place. Declan in that bed; Declan, whom she'd met backpacking through Europe the summer after her first year of university, and who had come to Toronto for the weekend, and then stayed, for her. And she, feeling nothing for him, had let him stay, thinking, the wound of Roman's departure open to the air but still unhealed, *If this is how people treat each other in this world, fine, that's what I'll do, too.* She'd let him stay after hearing him quit his job at a Dublin newspaper over Skype. After he told her, *Some things are too important not to make sacrifices for.* Estela remembered seeing him naked for the first time, his muscular torso and long, erect penis, his short-cropped hair and gentle, open face, the physical attraction she'd felt and been surprised by, the single candle he'd lit, his welcoming laugh as he'd stretched his arms out to her.

She defended herself to herself: *It's not like I made a commitment, he was never my boyfriend, I didn't ask him to come or to stay, he should have watched his own heart.*

Years later she would search for him on Facebook, first on her phone and then on a friend's, only to realize that, yes, he'd still blocked her.

Estela's letter from the Ontario Court of Appeal was waiting at her parents' house. It had arrived a week earlier—she'd put down their address on Grove in Old Ottawa South as her permanent one, given that she and Edgar had still been apartment hunting when she'd applied for the clerkship in her second year of law school—and it was still in their mail holder when she arrived on Good Friday, overnight bag in hand. In the front entrance, the house quiet, she tore open the envelope.

After reading the committee's official decision, Estela replaced the single white sheet back in the envelope, folded it in half, and tucked it in the back right pocket of her jeans. She walked into the kitchen, where her parents exclaimed their greetings and hugged her, her mother pulling lasagna out of the oven, her father leading her over to the kitchen table to show her the map of the cross-country trail he'd chosen for the following morning's ski in Gatineau Park. Neither she nor they brought up the letter or its contents.

During her articling interviews, when she'd had to defend the decision she'd made that night—to decline the clerkship—Estela always chose some variation of the truth: that she'd done so for family reasons.

In her interview at Davies, she said it was because of her maternal grandmother's Alzheimer's, the shock of the diagnosis, the need to spend a few months with her at her home in Mexico City before she declined further. To Osler, she said it was her father's prostate cancer, diagnosed early but still requiring regular trips to and from the Civic for treatment.

To no one she said, *I'd been managing since I was twelve, and suddenly I was not.* That after a decade and a half of barely staying afloat she'd lain back to rest and instead had sunk, had been crushed by the water's weight, its thousands of pascals of pressure. That she'd been drowning that Easter weekend at her parents' house, that lonely ocean's water having finally overwhelmed her lungs.

That every time Estela reached for something she desired—be it the clerkship at the court or the man sitting on the park bench across from hers in Paris, where she'd spent the summer after her third year of law school instead, her father's illness having occurred years before she'd claimed it had, her grandmother's over a year after—Ethan's spectre rose up to impede her, reminding her: *I never got to learn, I never got to love. Why should you?*

The man on the bench: What if he gave her a tight smile and looked away? What if they were to fall in love, become inseparable, walk hand in hand across the Pont Neuf on a starry night, and then one morning she awakes and he is gone, with a note—*I had to go back to her*—on the bedside table?

What if the first draft memorandum she delivered to her assigned justice came back with a comment declaring it to be shoddy work? What if she overheard him in his chambers—*She really is the worst clerk I've ever had*—through the solid oak-panelled door?

Estela lived hand-to-mouth, avoiding any blow she knew she wouldn't recover from, starting each morning as a video game fighter with her life bar in the red—as if she'd been half-depleted on November 12, 1994, and never recovered.

Estela met Edgar in her second year of law school, at a party, but didn't get to know him until they were both selected to moot. After three weeks of meeting nightly in their group of four, they started dating. By February, they'd moved in together.

Edgar was the perfect mate. He gave incredible foot massages. He cooked and baked and prepped her lunches alongside his in smart, divided Tupperware containers. He was intelligent—Estela had found the letter that renewed his entrance scholarship for a second year folded neatly in half and pressed between the pages of their shared copy of *The Criminal Code of Canada*, bookmarking the section on nuisances—but humble.

He was great in bed. He played the dominant partner even if it was a stretch for him, allowing Estela all of her favourite positions—him on top with her arms held over her head, or from behind but grasping her hips so tightly she couldn't move, then flattening her chest-down onto the bed as he came, as if she had no choice in the matter—every time they had sex.

Her father loved him. Early on, she'd invited Edgar to replace her parents' neighbour as their fourth euchre player for a night. Halfway through the game her father had whispered, *He's a keeper,* as they passed each other walking to and from the kitchen, and, over the course of the night, had poured Edgar at least three inches of his favourite Japanese whisky, which he rarely took out of the liquor cabinet.

Her friends loved him. In front of Callie, Estela's best friend from high school, whom he'd met when they'd joined her and her young daughter at a nearby park, he'd said, *I want to take as much leave as I can when I have kids*, this to the woman who'd refused to have a second child *because my husband won't even watch the one child we have for long enough for me to take a shower*, as she'd told Estela. *You, my friend, have hit the husband jackpot.*

Edgar was unselfish in everything he did. The morning registration opened for the fall semester, they'd sat across from one another at the dining room table, laptops out. Within seconds all sixty spots in Taxation were gone; Edgar had gotten one, Estela hadn't. Close to midnight that same day, he withdrew from the course so that she, moments later, could take his place. He'd give her the larger of the last two pieces of pie. At a restaurant, whenever he ordered something that turned out to be better, he'd switch plates with her.

And yet every kind gesture grated on Estela, caught on some sharp crag within her. So the day she came home late from the library to find Edgar watching TV on the couch, smiling happily as she entered and offering her popcorn, she slammed the front door behind her and went straight upstairs.

She hadn't been allowed to see Ethan. Her parents had gone over, leaving her with the neighbour, leaving her to imagine his bloated face, his mouth filled with fish, and his veins, blue and bulging, like spiderwebs. She remembered sitting twenty floors above Dundas in her tiny apartment and looking out over the abandoned lot, in her first year of graduate school, and realizing that Roman's first book on Milton employed *her* thesis, that he'd listened quietly to her critique and then rewritten it without telling her.

And so she'd thought, when Edgar looked up from the sofa and held his popcorn out to her, *Don't fucking offer me popcorn. Don't fucking offer me* everything. *This is not how the world is.*

After articling back in Toronto—chosen over Ottawa to escape Edgar, who'd proposed at the end of their third year and with whom she'd broken up shortly thereafter—she ended up at a small firm that practised estate law.

Estela had found the job through Jasper, who was a friend of Giselle's, Estela's best friend from graduate school. Estela and Jasper had in fact been matched twice: first by Tinder—she'd seen his cute bio, *Father of Two, Future Boyfriend of One*, and swiped right, breaking her rule about not dating older men with kids, only to have the text conversation languish—and then by Giselle, who set them up on a blind date.

Toward the end of the meal, he said, "You might like what I do. Estate law. It's all about relationships, and guiding the involved parties as well as you can when the emotional and financial stakes are high. And it happens that we're looking for a new associate."

"Well, maybe I'll apply," Estela replied.

Estela awoke to the sound of Jasper in the shower and to four text messages from Giselle. *So?* read the first; then *??*; then an eggplant emoji with a question mark; and then *Well, the fact that you're not awake yet probably tells me all I need to know. See you at ten.*

At brunch, Giselle laughed as soon as Estela sat down. "I knew you'd get along," she said.

"We did, but I doubt we'll see each other again," Estela said, looking down at the menu, which was attached to a clipboard.

"Why's that?"

"I just didn't really get a commitment vibe from him."

"Are you sure it wasn't him not getting a commitment vibe from you?"

"What do you mean?"

"Nothing," Giselle said. She was silent for a few seconds. "Well, only that any guy who'd be good for you, you have a one-night stand with or break up with, and anyone it couldn't possibly work out with gets your undying attention."

Giselle kept her eyes on the menu. Estela's mind jumped ahead to the moment at the end of the meal when the bill would arrive and she would pull out her credit card, suddenly a working professional sitting across from an impoverished PhD candidate, who would, then as now, avoid Estela's gaze. Estela hated this moment; she knew Giselle hated it more.

Estela poured her friend a glass of water from the carafe on the table. A waiter walked past carrying a stack of blueberry pancakes topped with whipped cream.

"I'm getting those," Estela said brightly.

"I'll have the same," Giselle said.

"About Jasper. About men," Estela said. "I'm not that bad, am I?"

Walking to the streetcar after brunch, her fall coat drawn around herself, Estela stopped at the window of a design store. A pair of button cufflinks had caught her eye, blue and made of enamel; she'd seen these before, with Ash, at a menswear boutique across town, when she'd first moved to Toronto. She'd planned to buy them for Ash's birthday, years ago—even though she wouldn't have been able to afford them at the time—but had then stopped speaking to him. She could afford them now.

During the streetcar ride home, Estela opened Facebook. For the hundredth time, she went to Ash's profile and flirted with the idea of hitting Add Friend, her thumb hovering over the blue button. She'd heard from a mutual friend that he'd been in Argentina but was now back in Ottawa, studying Chinese. Estela remembered the last time she'd seen him, having fled his apartment while he was still in the shower, her backpack slung over her shoulder, her rush down the building's stairs. She'd missed the ground floor and gone a half flight too far, pushing the fire door out onto Seventy-Second Street, then walking past a row of trash cans, disoriented.

The streetcar squealed against the tracks as it approached Spadina. She closed the app, pressed the side button on her phone, and slipped it back into her pocket.

The day she met Allister, she was a fourth-year associate with a packed morning schedule of meetings, to which he had been added right before lunch. The partner in charge of Allister's file had emailed Estela the night before, from Paris, and asked her to take the last-minute meeting in his stead.

Allister's request was straightforward: to redraft his will now that his ex-wife had remarried and stepped down as co-director of the charity they'd founded in memory of their son, who had died of cancer when he was eight.

"I've been sole director for four years, and yes, I'm only sitting down to do this with you now," he joked, after he was led into Estela's office by her assistant and he and Estela had been introduced.

"I mean, I have this one." He pulled out a sheet of lined paper that had clearly been torn from a notebook, scrawled on, and signed. "A holographic will, it's called?"

"Ha, yes," Estela said. "Though you definitely shouldn't keep your will in your wallet. That's my first piece of legal advice."

Allister laughed.

"Let's get started," Estela said, suddenly shy. Allister's knees were touching her desk and he stretched his legs out to accommodate them, his foot almost touching hers. He squinted against the bright sunlight that filtered through her window.

"Your last will became ineffective four years ago with your divorce. In it, you'd left half of your estate to the foundation, a third to your now ex-wife, and a sixth to your sister."

"Yes," Allister replied. "The big question for me now is how much to leave, if anything, to Sarah. My sister and the foundation are still in my good graces," he joked.

Estela laughed, moving her foot an inch closer to his under the table.

"Well, most people don't leave much, or anything, to ex-spouses," Estela said. "Though that's not to say you couldn't or shouldn't. It all depends on your relationship with her now, and how you think it will change in the future. Just remember that thirty-three percent that goes to her is thirty-three percent less that goes to—" She stopped short.

"Everything else," Allister finished for her. He paused for a moment. "After this, do you have time to have lunch in the park? Coffee and sandwiches are on me."

For six months after the new will was notarized—Allister had elected to maintain his ex-wife's third—Estela didn't hear from him, though she'd occasionally see his photo in *Toronto Life*, two or three times with the same woman, and, more recently, with someone new.

And then he called her.

"Hi," he said. "I have a question for you. Do you think it was weird that I did that?"

"Weird that you did what?" Estela replied, even though she knew.

"Left my ex-wife in my will."

"Not at all. Most people don't, but I can see how in particular situations it might be reasonable to do so."

"Come on, Estela," he teased, his voice warm and with a new lightness. "Tell me what you really think. I'm not your client anymore."

Estela quickly crossed Bay, ducking into a recessed doorway to escape the noise of the street, the cold of the December wind.

"Okay, fine," she said. "I did think it was weird. That was money that could have gone to your son's foundation. Or to your sister. Or that you could have used to buy a Lamborghini."

"I knew it!"

They both laughed.

"Have dinner with me?" Allister asked.

A year passed. Estela loved Allister's shape, his height in a crowd. That while he'd studied commerce at Queen's he'd preferred his second major, in philosophy. And that while he'd inherited his wealth—he was the great-great-grandson of a farming-implement magnate from Manitoba—he was also a good friend, a good citizen, generous.

He was a loyal partner, even in her absence. At a party, having returned to the front entrance to get her phone out of her coat pocket, she'd turned back just in time to see the blond news anchor, the one who'd gone to high school with Allister, touch his elbow and leave her hand there. Allister had allowed it for a few seconds before reaching out with the same arm to tap a passing partygoer on the shoulder, bringing him into their circle. When the same woman said, once Estela had rejoined them, *Though you're not really working as a lawyer anymore, are you?* Allister had interjected, before Estela could, *I don't see why she should have to stop*, and the woman had needled, *Children?*

Later that night, at the same party, Estela overheard him say, *I don't think I could have another one*, and, not knowing if he'd meant a cocktail, or—finding herself suddenly unable to breathe—a child, she'd gone up to the master bathroom, past the No Entry sign slung over the stairs, and sat on the closed toilet seat, only returning after Allister texted her, wondering where she was.

Their flight to Rome was delayed by four hours. They had a glass of wine each in the lounge, then wandered the terminal, bright squares of sunlight underfoot. During a pause in front of the floor-to-ceiling windows, looking out at what was likely their plane, Allister said, "Sarah's way of surviving Oliver's death was to try to forget he'd even existed." He paused for a moment. "I know that sounds harsh."

It was the first time he'd mentioned his ex-wife and his son by name in the same sentence. Estela waited. Allister briefly loosened his grip on her hand, then tightened his fingers around hers again. "Obviously, she wasn't successful in that. She'd seem fine for months and then overdose on sleeping pills. The first time, I heard the bathroom door lock and I knew immediately, immediately, what was happening. Never in the twenty years we'd been together did we ever lock the bathroom door. Sometimes Sarah left the door wide open to pee. So I banged on the door, forced her to open it, and made her throw up the pills."

An airline employee at the check-in counter announced four last names from the standby list. Allister remained quiet while the names were called again.

"The second time, she was with Arash. He told me about it, asked what he should do. And then he never called again after that. And she's still alive now, and they have a daughter together, so I guess she's okay."

Two seats became available nearby and so they sat, their backs to the windows and the tarmac, the length of their legs touching, holding hands. Across from them a young girl sat on her mother's lap, eating a chocolate croissant. A man and a woman with two teenage kids sat beside them, all four looking down at their phones.

"Is it hard to look at children? At families, together?" Estela asked.

"Yes," Allister said. "I wonder what Oliver would have been like at that age. And if the kid is younger, I remember what Oliver was like—how he was different, how he was the same. That little girl, for example," he said. "Oliver would have eaten around the edges and saved the chocolate seam in the middle for last."

"I am so sorry," Estela said. In the year and a half they'd been together there hadn't been the right time to say it, and that she hadn't yet had stuck like a pin in her chest. She reached across his lap for his other hand so that both of hers held both of his. The corners of his mouth turned upward slightly, briefly.

"Looking back, there was no way our marriage was going to make it. She was trying to forget in order to survive and I was trying to remember as much as I could. We had the same features, Oliver and I. He took after me exactly. Sometimes, if Sarah had managed to reach a moment of peace, if she'd truly forgotten for a second—mid-laughter with a friend, for example—she'd turn to me and her face would just crumple. She'd just look so stunned. I'm surprised she lasted as long as she did."

Their flight was called. Allister turned to Estela, squinting in the bright light, reminding her of the day they'd met.

"I know it doesn't make sense to keep Sarah in my will. She doesn't even know she's still in it. And I will take her out eventually," he said, squeezing Estela's palm. "I'm just not ready yet. It's the last remaining connection to the family we were, and dissolving that bond is up to me. It's the only thing that's up to me. All the rest—our photos, Oliver's toys, his drawings—Sarah cleaned everything out."

They remained seated long after their boarding zone had been called, only standing to join the line after the waiting area had emptied. Allister held Estela close to him, his arm around her shoulders, all the way down the jet bridge and onto the plane, only separating from her when they walked down the aisle to their seats.

A few days after her thirty-fifth birthday, panicked by the milestone, Estela downloaded a fertility tracker and went to the drugstore to buy ovulation sticks. She hid the plastic-wrapped wands in their guest bathroom between two boxes of tampons. The app she aimed to conceal in a folder on her iPhone, but halfway through the download—she'd been in a café, out of its Wi-Fi zone but too far inside to use her phone's data—it stopped.

Estela had been having lunch with Calliope. Calliope, a younger lawyer, had been her mentee for four years, and had just failed a third round of IVF. Hana, a friend from high school, thirty-five like her, had just had two miscarriages, one in the second trimester when they'd detected a fetal anomaly. Wei, who was forty and a colleague at Estela's firm, had been trying for years with no success and had just been told by her doctor that if she didn't freeze her eggs right now, she soon wouldn't have that option either.

"I know most women in their thirties have no trouble having children," Calliope said, piercing a cherry tomato and a sprig of arugula with her fork. "So how is it that everyone I know is having a hard time?"

Estela didn't answer and left the rest of her salad untouched. And later, when Calliope went to the bathroom because she'd forgotten to check the consistency of her cervical mucus that morning, Estela searched for and started to download the app, hurriedly sliding her phone back in her purse when Calliope returned.

It was in this frozen state, brightly coloured up to the seven o'clock position, that Allister found the app icon on the home screen of Estela's phone.

"What's this?" he asked.

He was in the kitchen in front of a pot of simmering chicken broth, still wearing the suit and tie from his afternoon meeting, the top button of his shirt undone. Steam fogged his reading glasses as he looked down at her phone, which he'd borrowed seconds earlier to convert ounces to grams for the morels.

"Is this a pregnancy app?"

She crossed the kitchen and he turned the phone to her, reading out loud what was visible of the app's title: Ovulation and Peri—. Estela became aware of the sound of the stock for the risotto bubbling beside them, conscious suddenly of how Allister towered over her as he extended his arm to show her the screen, the phone less than a foot from her face. His tone was hard and incredulous. Estela felt as if she'd just walked into a glass door she hadn't known was there.

She took her phone and stepped back. "Oh, that's a period tracker," she said. "My periods have been all over the place lately. Dr. Raza asked me to keep a calendar."

It was the closest they'd come to talking about it, and her request had died, unborn, in her throat.

Estela couldn't have built a happier life. She and Allister lived together in Allister's three-storey, five-bedroom house in Rosedale. She loved her work, which she now did part-time and half from home, drafting trust deeds and memoranda on an antique desk in a sunny nook that faced out toward the garden. She did yoga three times a week and had befriended the instructor at her studio, going out for brunch with her after almost every class. She kept up with old friends, too, going to plays and wine bars on the weekends, and on overnight trips to Montreal or New York. She was close with her parents, who called her weekly from their land line, their voices as soft and solicitous with each other as with her.

And yet, even in brightest June, in the early morning when they sat across from each other with their coffee, and Allister would show her a *New Yorker* cartoon and she would laugh, there was a part of him that remained concealed in the long shadow of winter. As if the skin she touched every day were a shell, not his real skin, a carapace he hid under.

It was only at night, lying beside him—awoken suddenly by the change in rhythm of his breath, or by some other instinct—that she saw that guarded part of him exposed. She'd hear him breathe, faster and more varied than during sleep, and pretend not to notice he was awake. Awake, and alone, and absent from their life together.

Allister had noted her new subscription to *Cook's Illustrated* and signed them up for culinary classes. He'd flown in her three best friends for her thirty-fifth birthday dinner. He watched her favourite films with her—usually *Atonement* or *Legends of the Fall*—and held her against his chest when she cried. But all this he did with his attention potentially withdrawn at any moment, at any given second that glazed look in his eye that meant he was back at nine years ago, at Oliver's bedside, or searching through databases of oncology trials in the States, or driving with Sarah to yet another grief counsellor, then yet another marriage counsellor.

The look that told Estela that right when she had everything, she in fact had nothing.

Four years to the day after they'd met, Allister took Estela back to Berczy Park, where he'd placed two Tim Hortons double-doubles on the fountain edge.

Estela dropped his hand and laughed. "That's what you were doing while I was waiting in the car?"

"They're probably not hot anymore. They're likely just for show at this point," Allister joked.

"To be completely accurate, we'd have to spill half of one on my skirt."

"Did you do that?"

"Well, almost. I was so nervous. I was worried I'd make a terrible impression."

"You made a very good impression," he said, brushing her hair off her cheek and cupping the side of her face with his palm.

Estela sat beside one of the coffee cups, and Allister did the same, facing her.

"I brought you here to ask you something," Allister said. "But there's something else I wanted to talk about. First. Something we've been avoiding."

Estela was silent. The sun was warm on her knees. A dog ran by with a red Frisbee in its mouth.

"Do you want children? Because..." He paused. "I—I can't again. I can't start over like that. I will give you all my love but I can't. So if that's important to you, if it's a deal-breaker, we shouldn't do this."

For the first time in years, Estela thought of the abortion she'd had when she was twenty. She wished—regardless of what other consequences there might have been, regardless of the fact that those consequences would have been, for her, worse—that she'd had that baby. That way no one could tell her, at the age of thirty-six, that she had to choose between love and being a mother.

"I do," Estela said. Allister's face sagged, and Estela, for a second, was furious. How could he know so little about her, to not know the answer to that question? To have been ready to propose contingent on a response he should have known he was never going to receive? She was also angry at herself: how had *she* not brought this up in their four years together?

Even though she knew why: Allister's still-lowered voice whenever he spoke his son's name, the weekly phone call with his sister that he took behind the closed door of his study, his old grief like a worn stone, a grief in which she could not participate.

"I've always wanted kids," Estela said. "For as long as I can remember. Especially with what happened to my brother."

She looked up at Allister. Their eyes met for a second, and then Estela looked down at her hands, in her lap. "It's not that I think I can replace Ethan. But we've been moorless, my family and I, since he died, and this is the only way I know how to fix it. I can give them a grandchild. I can have my own, intact family, with a mom and a dad and one or two kids. I can restart. I think I'm more like Sarah than you in this way."

Allister looked up in surprise at his ex-wife's name.

"We were a happy family, and then he died, and we were just three miserable individuals. My parents have each other. I have no one."

The fountain's spray thundered in Estela's ears, sprinkling the back of her neck with tiny droplets. She stood.

"I guess this is it, then?"

After she and Allister broke up, Estela moved in with Giselle. She realized, as she unpacked, that she now had half of everything: half of their books, though some were hers and some were Allister's; half of their coffee machine, which meant that neither of them could make coffee; all of the hand towels but none of the bath towels. She'd walked out of the shower one morning wearing three small terry cloth rectangles, and Giselle had laughed. *Welcome back to the single life, my friend*, she'd said, not unkindly.

Her resolve not to google him weakened only once—for one single day—but the image she saw stayed with her forever: Allister, in a three-piece suit with a bow tie, his head turned to the side, laughing, the beautiful Vietnamese woman on his arm, her lavender dress with the plunging neckline, she looking straight into the camera. Estela instantly memorized the caption: *Divorcees out on the town: Allister Tiessen and Mai-Anh Nguyen at TIFF's B.L.A.C.K. Ball.*

The day before Naomi, Roman's second ex-wife, called, Estela had been going through the single remaining box of clothes she'd left at her parents' house, at her mother's request. In it she found the black satin, lace-hemmed skirt she'd worn all through that summer between her third and fourth years at McGill, the summer she'd spent with Roman, the summer she'd turned down planting trees in the Rockies with Ash for.

The skirt was neatly folded between two binders of notes. Those four months had gone by in a haze of sun and wine, hands intertwined under the tables of comedy clubs, evenings spent with her head on Roman's lap and her nose in a book, reading the words he'd underlined. But Estela saw now, at thirty-six, that she'd been caught in his eddy, at twenty, and that the life she could have lived—a July kiss after a hard day digging holes for saplings, meeting Ash's parents, as she never had, counting on his loving support while she struggled to make tenure—had gone on without her, hurtling downstream.

That same day, she'd received the email reply from Ash detailing the letter his would-be fiancée had left him, the email written in the late-night, confidential tone she hadn't had from him in years.

So when Naomi called to tell Estela about the sexual harassment claim she'd filed with McGill, when she asked Estela to go from rival to co-conspirator to truth teller to #MeToo advocate, Estela said yes, angry, at just that instant, for the life Roman had had her miss.

"This is going to be superawkward, but I need your help," Estela said to Ash. She cleared her throat and pressed the phone to her ear. "Do you remember Roman?"

"I remember the era of Roman, certainly," Ash replied.

"Well, I need you to write a statement corroborating my version of events."

"What?"

"For a university hearing. I'm saying he abused his position of power over me by sleeping with me while I was his student," she said. "Basically, I finally agree with you."

Ash was silent.

"I'm not the main complainant," Estela said quickly. "The main complainant, so to speak, is his ex-wife. Also a former student."

Estela cut through Saint-Louis Square. It was a bright, cold March day; she'd gone right from her parents' house in Ottawa to Montreal, for a conference at Concordia. To her right, a father and his daughter kicked a small soccer ball back and forth through the mud, over scattered piles of snow.

"But you were in love with him," Ash said. "You were with him, if we can call it that, for over a year."

"Yes, I was in love with him," Estela said. "And yes, we were having sex consensually over the course of that year. But did I have sex with him and was I in love with him because of that power differential?" She paused. "You're supposed to be on my side."

"I am on your side," Ash said. "I was on your side through all of it, remember?"

Estela heard him shift the phone from one ear to the other, then sigh.

"What do you want me to say?" he asked.

ALLISTER

He hadn't done it to be famous, but he'd recognized the Audi with the vanity plate, RAD ONC, and gone back to his SUV to get his shovel. And when a pediatrics resident he knew unlocked the door two cars behind the staff oncologist's, he dug her out, too. And then he liberated the car in between them, his goose-down jacket now tossed onto the hood of the resident's car, after learning it belonged to a nurse.

There was a write-up in the *Star—Dad Digs Out SickKids Staff from Blizzard*—but when he'd seen it he'd folded the newspaper quietly and hadn't shown Sarah. He received calls all day, from friends but also from journalists, even a producer from CBC Radio who wanted to interview him. To them all he responded ambivalently, he declined.

Allister had last seen Mai-Anh, his sister's best friend, on his wedding day, so it was with a jolt—of surprise, of pleasure—that he noticed her email in his inbox.

Mai-Anh Nguyen-Saccomani

(no subject)

I saw the article in the Star. *I'm sorry I didn't write before.*

I...

He noted the new double-barrelled last name. He clicked on the message, even though there were three or four earlier unread emails, and scanned the rest: *...can't even imagine what you're going through. Big hugs to you and Sarah, and to Oliver, of course. I know we're not the closest of friends but if you ever need anything, just ask.*

At his wedding, he'd run into her, wearing a green dress with a peacock-feather motif, near the hors d'oeuvres table. He'd turned, wineglass in hand, mid-laughter from something his best man had said, and she'd been there. A waiter had walked past then with a tray of champagne flutes, and he'd grabbed one, just to have something to do with his left hand, which, faced with her, had suddenly seemed extraneous, in need of purpose.

She'd raised her eyebrows at this.

"For Sarah," he'd said.

He remembered the day they'd gone to the mall together, looking for decorations for his sister's twenty-seventh birthday party. His sister had wanted LEGO blocks formed into cubes and glued together in groups of three. *Three cubes for turning three cubed. It's because she's an engineer that she finds this hilarious,* he'd said, as they stepped onto a down escalator at the Eaton Centre. *Your dad would have loved it, too,* Mai-Anh had said.

At this he'd turned from her, a sharp sound in his throat, bringing his hands to his face. And she'd held him, her arms tight around his chest from behind, her mouth against his neck, the point of her nose cold still from the December wind.

Allister told Mai-Anh he loved her, two years later, while drunk at a house party. He'd been leaning against a door frame, next to a buddy of his, and she'd been standing nearby, having just broken away from a group of her friends to say hi to him. He'd said, *You know that I love you, right?* and his friend had said, *What, dude?* knowing that he was with Sarah.

He'd meant it: not an *I love you* to take her home that night, or make her his girlfriend instead, or marry her or regret not marrying her, but an *I love you* that acknowledged that moment on the escalator when she had seen him, and he had let himself be seen by her.

An *I love you*, however, that had made him avoid her, going forward, the moment he'd said his vows.

It had started innocuously enough, after Oliver had tripped over a raised tuft of grass playing soccer. He'd limped off the field, and he continued to limp even after tearing through the orange quarters provided by another parent as halftime refreshments.

The next day, despite Advil, and ice, and a Tensor bandage wrapped around his right knee in figure eights, the pain was still there.

When Oliver was still limping a week later, Allister took him to an urgent care clinic where a laughing, jocular pediatrician palpated his knee, flexed and extended it, and then had him walk down the hallway. When his leg flew up as the doctor tapped his knee with his reflex hammer, Oliver turned and grinned at his father.

When they returned from X-ray, the pediatrician's face was sombre, and even as he said, *Sometimes these tumours are benign*, Allister saw that he didn't mean it, saw in the single instance the doctor raised his eyes to meet his the months and months of misery that stretched ahead for them. Allister had asked, *Can we go home to get a change of clothes, a few games, before we go to the ER?* The doctor had shaken his head. *No, better to go right there.*

From the clinic, Allister realized later, he should have called a taxi. On his way to SickKids he failed to see a car changing lanes at the same time he did, and ran a red light while looking ahead to the next one, which had been green.

Oliver had been cold while waiting to be seen in the ER. A nurse brought him a blanket, not for the last time.

When they left the ER, it was with a diagnosis of a right distal femoral osteosarcoma, and appointments with oncology and orthopedics for the next day. They also left with crutches; Allister didn't know it then, but his proud little boy, lover of Messi and Ronaldo, projected star forward of Team Canada 2026, as they often joked, would never walk again.

During Oliver's hospital admission, Sarah sat by his bedside during the day and slept by his bedside at night on the parent chair that folded out flat into a daybed. She'd decorated the room with colourful bedspreads and throw pillows, posters and flowers, and his most portable toys, his Rubik's Cube and magician set. Sometimes Allister slept in the makeshift bed without her—giving her a chance to go home, take a shower, and rotate Oliver's selection of books—and sometimes they both slept in it together, a horrendous parody of when they'd done this as teenagers, in their first year of university, in each other's dorm rooms.

Allister's grandmother—who was in her nineties and familiar with hospitals from a decade earlier when Allister's grandfather had been admitted with pancreatic cancer—also visited, sitting tight-lipped in a corner when the medical team came by on rounds, writing out her questions. She told Oliver their family history, of her half-brother who'd gone off to war and died of typhus; of how, after anarchists had run through the Mennonite settlements of Ukraine, the rest of the family had taken the train to Riga, then travelled to Southampton by boat, and then on to Quebec City, and finally, by train again, to Kitchener, covered in lice and speaking only German; of her years on the assembly line at the Heinz factory in Leamington, Ontario, and how she passed the time between labelling a bottle and waiting for the next one by reading poetry—Wordsworth in her right apron pocket, and Heine, in German, in her left shirt pocket, over her heart.

While Oliver slept, which was often, Allister's grandmother crocheted him a blanket of yellow wool. By the time Oliver died, it had become long and wide enough to cover a grown man—as if, clear-eyed and practical in everything, having survived a girlhood in which there were often only turnips, if anything, to eat, an adolescence of raids and wars, and then eight decades as an immigrant in a new land—as if only now, she allowed herself denial, refused to see the truth.

It was back at home, still bedridden but in good spirits, his last white count reasonably high, that Oliver started to cough. Allister and Sarah checked the list the doctors had given them of symptoms to watch for—bone pain, any firm mass, cough or difficulty breathing—even though they had them all memorized, even though they already knew.

They took Oliver back to the emergency room at SickKids, all wearing masks.

His white count was fine. A CT of his lungs showed the metastases.

They stayed in the hospital for six weeks for another round of chemo and radiation therapy, this time targeting the lesions in his chest. Allister alternated between visiting his son at SickKids and running across the street to see his grandmother, who had been admitted at Mount Sinai; he'd kiss her cheek on arrival and she'd whisper, *Go, leave, go to Oliver.*

Then, one night, Oliver got a fever; his counts had dropped; they gave him PipTazo, they added vancomycin, they added an antifungal agent. When his heart raced and his blood pressure dropped, they put him on an epinephrine drip and transferred him to the ICU. And then, twelve hours later, he was gone.

Leaving the hospital was a blur. What Allister remembered most was Sarah, sitting in the back of the car, sobbing over the new books she'd ordered that had just arrived in the mail: *Diary of a Wimpy Kid* and *The Lightning Thief.*

ASH

The last night of their friendship—until Estela resumed emailing Ash out of the blue almost fourteen years later, and then called him with her request about Roman a few months after that—was on a November weekend, when he was a graduate student in international affairs at Columbia. Estela had been doing her MA in Toronto; they'd been speaking weekly, and Ash had repeatedly suggested that she visit him, until she finally did.

Ash took the bus to LaGuardia to meet her flight. When Estela appeared through the arrival doors, dressed in a black sweater and loose floral pants that tied around her waist, her hair wild from the plane, he'd been looking for her so hard he almost didn't register that he'd seen her. His love for her so far outstripped the reality of their relationship, as close as they were, that he felt fortunate she even considered him her friend, let alone that she had bought a ticket and set aside the time and was now before him.

Ash had planned their days together down to the minute: first brunch at a smoked-fish place on the Upper West Side, then dropping Estela's backpack off at his apartment before heading down to MoMA and Central Park, then dinner with a mutual friend who had just started as an analyst at Morgan Stanley. For Sunday, he'd planned a morning of gallery-hopping in Chelsea, then brunch at a Georgian restaurant on Fourteenth Street, after which he'd accompany her back on the M60 to catch her plane.

They never made it to the second day. As they were walking home from dinner, all the way up Broadway from the Village, Estela said, "My brother died, eleven years ago today."

"I didn't know," Ash replied, aghast, unheard over the traffic.

"My grandmother died two years later. On the same date. She overdosed on barbiturates. He'd been at her house—she'd been babysitting—but he snuck out the back door while she was doing laundry and drowned in the pond behind her house."

"Oh my God," Ash whispered.

"Why wasn't I babysitting? I was twelve, he was seven, I could have. I was at ringette practice. Ringette."

The next morning, while Ash was in the shower, Estela left.

But, deep down, Ash had known. He and Estela had been in McLennan, in December of their third year, studying for exams. Ash had rushed back to their shared desk on the fourth floor, cellphone in hand, cheeks red from the cold.

"Hey, Stel, I need your credit card," he said. "Mine declined. The guy's waiting at the door."

"Here," she said, reaching over protein bar wrappers and sheets of loose-leaf paper for her wallet. "I'll be down in a sec. Last paragraph." Ash jogged to the exit doors to take the stairs back to the main floor.

After paying for their pizza, Ash found himself flipping through the cards in Estela's wallet. Her Ontario health card. Two bank cards, one for TD, one for Scotia. Two loyalty cards with ten stamps each. A photograph of a boy, dressed in a school uniform and wearing a tan backpack over both shoulders, his hands clasped in front of him, the start of a smile, cheerful eyes.

Ash held the photo out to Estela when she came down to meet him in the library foyer, the only place in the building where food was allowed.

"This fell out," he said, when he'd in fact almost not seen the photo—sandwiched as it had been between her driver's licence and her Metro card—and had had to sneak it out with his fingernails.

Estela was quiet. "That's my brother, Ethan," she said, finally. She took the photo back from Ash and slid it back into place in her wallet, then sat down beside him and picked up her pizza box.

Estela said nothing further, and she didn't mention Ethan again.

After New York they'd had no contact, even though at one point they were both living in Ottawa, mere blocks from one another, in the Glebe. Ash had seen Estela only once, coming out of the Bridgehead near Second Avenue, her latte wrapped in a holiday-themed knitted sleeve, and watched her climb onto the 7. He'd turned to face the bus as it drove by, and, for a second, they'd locked eyes through the window.

For a week after, he'd repeatedly checked his inbox and his texts, but there was nothing. It was through an acquaintance from graduate school in New York—Edgar—that Ash found out that Estela was at the University of Ottawa, studying law, as he was in her class.

"Wait, my Estela is your Estela?" Edgar had asked. "We're in torts together. She's brilliant."

"What do you mean, your Estela?" Ash asked.

"It's just a phrase, man," Edgar said.

Ash didn't see Edgar for years thereafter either. And, much later, when Ash and Estela finally became Facebook friends, he saw that she, for their second and third years of law school, had, in fact, become his Estela.

Despite his awareness that he and Estela lived in the same city, that they'd been fortunate enough to be thrown together again only to take no advantage of it whatsoever, the year Ash spent in Ottawa was a peaceful one. He'd gotten a job with the Canadian government as a foreign service officer. He lived alone, for the first time, in a one-bedroom apartment on O'Connor. He cycled to and from the language school in Gatineau where he was studying Spanish. Every morning he brewed coffee on the stove, sitting at his back window as the early-morning sunlight shifted across the blue-and-white Portuguese tiles of the shared courtyard. At night, he watched the Argentine equivalent of *Family Feud*, *100 argentinos dicen*, on YouTube and memorized vocabulary: moto, casco, guantes, tatuajes.

He reconnected with Estela's friends, the ones from high school who'd come to visit her on weekends when she was at McGill, and whom Ash had also befriended. He did this to be able to say, when they asked if he were going to Estela's birthday drinks, or to her boyfriend's potluck, or, once, his dismay like a fist in his throat, to "the baby shower at Estela's," before he realized it was for a friend, not Estela herself: *Oh, I had no idea, Estela and I really aren't that close anymore*. To be able to say her name out loud to someone else who knew her.

Even if, at the end of these exchanges, he always felt worse.

One spring Saturday, Ash got home from the gym to find his younger brother, Nik, sitting on his doorstep.

"The keys weren't under the flowerpot," Nik said.

"Sorry about that," Ash said, his last syllable buried in the wool of his brother's shoulder as they hugged. "A little overdressed, are we?"

"You know how it is. You spend a winter in India and you forget the winter you've known your whole life."

Ash laughed and nodded, but it had been years since he'd been in India. Not since he was fourteen and had snuck out of his aunt's house during her mid-afternoon nap, the summer sun searing his shoulders, and found himself walking down an alleyway, alone, hot dust gathering around his sandalled feet. It had been quiet away from the road, and he'd seen the neighbours' servant boy, with his longish curly black hair and thick eyelashes, asleep on a back stoop. Ash, disarmed by the disarray of his surroundings, the sudden silence, his body sluggish as if wading through knee-deep snow, had reached out to touch the sleeping boy's lips only to have his forearm slapped down roughly from behind. It was his cousin, Sanjay, who was eighteen and almost a foot taller than him; Sanjay spent the time he wasn't at school or studying for his engineering entrance exams peppering Ash with the facts about Canada he'd found in the family's encyclopedia and memorized. "We don't do that," Sanjay had said, seeing right through him, knowing why Ash had wanted to touch the boy before Ash had even known it himself.

Years later, when Sanjay died showing off for a girl riding on the back of his motorcycle, the arc of his U-turn too tight as he sped back to where her friends were waiting, his helmetless skull slamming against the concrete divider as the wheels skidded out from under them, Ash had been sad, of course. He'd remembered, suddenly, a fact he'd learned that summer, his last summer in India, a statistic to combat the barrage of statistics his cousin had shot at him, eager to know what Ash knew, to level the playing field, be equal to his cousin from the West: that every four minutes someone in India dies in a motor vehicle accident. And then Ash had felt relief. Because he'd never known, up until the day Sanjay died, whether Sanjay would out him.

"How is everyone?" Ash asked Nik, unlocking and then opening the front door.

"Good. They asked about you. About whether or not you're married yet."

"Ha," Ash said, taking a handful of letters from his mailbox before starting up the stairs to his apartment.

Ash had skipped the last three family trips to India. The first, when he was eighteen, he'd ducked out of with the excuse of a summer intensive program at a Scottish castle, one "designed to ensure success in the liberal arts at the university level." During the second, when he was twenty-two, he'd needed to move to New York, which had involved multiple trips to the IKEA in Paterson, New Jersey, to furnish his small Upper West Side apartment. For the third trip, he hadn't been asked for an explanation at all.

"Mom and Dad are planning to fly back through Delhi and Toronto instead of Vancouver so we can meet them in Toronto for the weekend," Nik said, walking into the living room ahead of his brother and collapsing onto the sofa. "What do you think?"

"Sounds great," Ash said. "What do you want first? A shower? A nap? Something to eat?"

"Definitely sleep," Nik said.

After Sanjay's accident—Ash had been in Calgary visiting his family when they'd gotten the call, and he had helped his mother open the series of emails, each with a small section of the CT of his cousin's brain, because while the neurosurgeon in Bangalore had already given his prognosis, the family had wanted Ash's mother, their brilliant sister who was now a doctor in the West, to take a second look—Ash realized he still had no interest in returning to India. *It's so hot*, he thought. *Why go in the summer when it's finally nice here?* When a winter trip was proposed, he thought: *I can't even understand anyone. I speak one word of Telugu. What's the point?* As his cousins grew up, added him on MySpace, and became obviously fluent English speakers, Ash, out of excuses, admitted the truth: that he didn't know who he was when he was in India, and that his parents didn't know who they were either, having by that point spent as many years outside their homeland as they'd spent in it. His parents were unrecognizable in Hyderabad, his mother suddenly docile and his father edging on boorish, each moving closer to who they felt their families expected them to be, away from themselves, away from him.

After Nik woke from a two-hour nap and Ash dragged him out for fried chicken, the brothers lay head to foot in Ash's double bed, the way they had when they were kids. Nik had returned from India a few days early to give his body clock time to adjust before his job interview at Ubisoft later that week, and, despite his earlier nap, fell asleep first. Ash listened to his slow breaths in and out; the duvet shifted slightly with the rise and fall of his brother's chest. He decided: *I will go to India again, one day, on my own terms.*

And then, right before he fell asleep, Ash realized he never would. Because another hesitation was buried below the one he'd recently uncovered: how to face his aunt, knowing that when her son died, it was as if the stones Ash had sewn into his pockets had suddenly been cut loose, had suddenly fallen away?

Ash continued to watch reruns of *100 argentinos dicen*, but now on cable TV in his Buenos Aires apartment. There was a telephone on a stool at the front entrance with a voice-messaging system Ash had yet to figure out. The other day, sick with a cold, he'd been so tired of struggling in Spanish that he'd said to the grocer, *Just give me lettuce, tomatoes, and some carrots,* and had left with two out of the three.

He was dating a man. Ash had met him at a Thanksgiving celebration hosted by one of his American counterparts in a beautiful high-ceilinged apartment with nineteenth-century mouldings in Palermo. They'd been seated next to each other at dinner, the wines from Mendoza, the chickens small and flavourful, with cans of cranberry sauce smuggled in from the States set down the length of the table.

"I'm Ash," he'd said. "I'm on the commercial side at the Canadian Embassy."

"Ash," Andrés had said. "Is that short for something?"

"Ashish," Ash had replied.

At the end of that first night, they left the dinner party together alongside a handful of the other guests. On Nicaragua, they lost a couple to a jazz club. On Paraguay, they lost another to a twenty-four-hour bookstore. Then it was just the two of them, on the streets of Buenos Aires at midnight, and when Andrés brushed his hand against Ash's forearm—by accident, or perhaps not—Ash used his other hand to hold it there, then intertwined their fingers.

Andrés was not without his flaws. One winter evening in July, they'd been at a barbecue in a gated community just outside Buenos Aires. His arms crossed below his chest, leaning back in his chair, Andrés had replied, when one of his best friends had hooted *What about Antonio?* to Andrés's claim that he'd never cheated on anyone: *That doesn't count. Antonio unilaterally decided we were long-distance for the summer. I wasn't consulted; I was told. I had no choice in the matter, so I hardly think what I did while he was in Pittsburgh counts as cheating.*

Once, Ash had crossed town, all the way from Belgrano to San Telmo, to meet Andrés in front of El Niño Bien. When he arrived—twenty minutes late, as his first taxi had bumped into a BMW at a red light and the driver of the latter had stepped out of his car, irate, and Ash had opted to flag down a second one—he found the stairs outside the handsome yellow stone building empty. Ash texted, *I travel from one end of the city to the other to meet you, and you just leave without even telling me?* Andrés answered immediately: *I told you, I don't wait for people. It's really disrespectful to be late.*

But it was a relationship with a man, which, after years of not being with men—of, instead, stalking the boys he'd been attracted to in high school on Facebook, friending them out of curiosity, and then unfriending them out of embarrassment—is what counted.

Andrés's critical nature did end up improving Ash's life, in one instance: Andrés's ruthless verbal pursuit of him when Ash revealed over dinner one night that he hadn't yet come out to anyone back home.

"You mean to say that you're twenty-six and from Canada, one of the best countries in the world to be gay—sorry, bi—and you're still in the closet?" Andrés said, when Ash told him that his parents would be visiting and that he wasn't ready for Andrés to meet them. To Ash's credit, this was because he doubted the relationship would last, not because he didn't want to tell his parents he was bi, and had made a quick calculation mid-conversation about which excuse would hurt less. It turned out not to matter.

"So, I have a reason for this," Ash said. He paused while a waiter cleared their plates. "Overall, you're right. Yes, I should have come out. I used my genuine attraction to women as a shield the way a gay man couldn't. I was wrong. But it wasn't as easy as you're suggesting to be a bi Indian kid. I think my immigrant parents might—*might*—have gotten gay. Bi would be pretty nebulous for them."

Ash then pointed out that Andrés was the son of liberal-minded parents whose daughter had already come out to them as a lesbian before Andrés hit puberty, and that he'd grown up in San Francisco, for God's sake, speaking of easy places to grow up gay.

They'd walked home from dinner in silence under the sweet-smelling purple jacaranda flowers of austral November, all the way down Cabildo toward Belgrano until they parted ways on Olleros, Ash turning right, Andrés turning left. The whole way back they'd walked two feet apart, not even needing to pretend to be just friends.

The first time Ash almost said something was when Estela had told him, sitting across from him at a wine bar on du Parc, in their second year of university: *I'm pretty sure that guy was checking you out.*

Ash had scoffed at her, even as he'd gripped his own thigh under the table. He'd wanted to say, *He was, and it was me who started it.*

But he didn't, just in case one day it made the difference between Estela choosing him or not.

Ironically, and out of a sense of injustice toward his parents—who, when Ash was six, insisted they'd arrange for him to marry a nice Hindu girl from Hyderabad; then, when he was twelve, widened the net to include nice South Indian girls who'd been raised in the West; then, at sixteen, broadened further to allow a love match from anywhere in India; and then, finally, after Ash had left home and flatly refused their suggestion to post an ad on Shaadi.com, had said, *Well, just find someone kind, who loves you back*—Ash actually did tell his parents he was bi during their trip to Buenos Aires.

Among the items Ash and Andrés had to split after their breakup: their diplomat friends, the native English speakers who banded together and celebrated the same holidays—Christmas, Easter, Thanksgiving—with the Americans going to Andrés and those from the relevant Commonwealth countries—Britain, Canada, and Australia—going to Ash; Andrés got their tango friends, including their instructor, Mauro, but Ash got their studio; Ash got the restaurants, bars, and parks west of Plaza Serrano, Andrés the ones to the east.

They met again only once, by accident, on a Friday—Ash had been given Saturday, Sunday, and Monday, Andrés Tuesday, Wednesday, and Thursday—at the gay milonga La Marshall, which had been considered neutral ground, a sort of no man's land. Ash had looked across the room at Andrés, who'd been in a stranger's arms, leading; Ash had nodded, briefly, and Andrés had nodded back.

Neither took the gesture to mean what it usually implied, that is, an invitation to dance. And for a second, no more, Ash missed their tango classes together at the studio on Córdoba and Corrientes—he, the shorter, following, the air dusty with the chalk from their feet, Andrés's chest pushing him into a giro con boleo, the sweat from his collarbone against Ash's cheek.

Ash was back in Gatineau, at the language school, one floor down from where he'd been three years before, studying Spanish. This time, he was taking Mandarin.

There were two other first-year Chinese classes—a Taiwan-specific one and one for francophones—and the students all compared notes at lunch, discovering that, at least for the first few weeks, they'd covered the same material: *I am a student, you are a teacher. My name is Ash, I am twenty-eight years old, I am from Canada.*

He chose a Chinese name—柯梣—and learned to write it out by hand.

He stayed up late into the night memorizing characters, the thousands of them, by rote, his keystrokes coinciding with the brush strokes of Chinese schoolchildren half a world away.

He felt the joy of reading books in a new language, of listening to music he'd heard before but not understood, of being able to text his former babysitter in Mandarin and receive her astounded reply.

Mandarin was one floor up from Portuguese, and as Ash passed the fledgling lusophones on his way out of the building—hearing their complete, fluid, accentless sentences while he tried not to screw up the difference between cǎo and cào—he thought of how different his life would be if he'd listed his second choice first and ended up as a trade commissioner in Rio. He remembered the work trip he'd taken there with a colleague, the photo of him in dark sunglasses with his arm around her shoulder, the one-night stand they'd had and the weekend they'd spent together after, blowing off the conference to walk hand in hand through the city, her suggestion that they try to get posted there together.

Through the glass pane in the door of the Portuguese classroom, Ash would see that same colleague, sitting in the front row, head bent, reciting along with the rest: Vou levar meia dúzia de ovos, por favor.

Nobody understood why he'd wanted to go to Beijing. *They're racist toward Indians*, Nik had said. *Why would you even bother with that?* His parents: *Isn't the air pollution worse than in Delhi?* A friend's partner at a random party, a partner he'd just met: *Don't you think your very presence there is a silent endorsement of their police state?*

There was truth to all of this. Beijingers looking through him, over him, unsmiling. Red-arm-banded citizens everywhere, watching everyone. Staying inside his apartment for four days straight when the air quality was poor, then watching from his window as an easterly wind swept the smog away, the air quality index dropping from 300 to 250 to below 100, then grabbing his keys and changing into shorts and going for a run, a gift, outside. Until thirty minutes later, when, stopped at a traffic light five kilometres from home, he'd checked the AQI again, noticed it was back over 200, and had to walk the hour home, his N95 on, in the cold.

And then there was the day he'd returned home from work to find his couch pillows arranged symmetrically and his desktop computer askew, back at the log-in screen.

But it was wondrous, too. Bicycles everywhere. A feeling of movement, of endless possibility, in all directions. He'd had some of the best food he'd ever eaten: the chicken-and-egg sandwich from his street corner (Ash always had the same joke for the seller, made in his foreigner's Mandarin: Xiān yǒu jī háishì xiān yǒu jidàn? Which came first, the chicken or the egg?); the Chinese versions of eggplant and cauliflower, more flavourful than their Western counterparts, that he bought at the farmers' market. The bar that popped up in a hutong one-storey and its award-winning mixologist from Japan, until the city authorities bricked it over. The extremes of people he met: the Danish journalist who always spoke of his overnight conquests' dainty shoes; the taxi driver who insisted the government was building a bridge to Vancouver.

He'd bike home from a brunch with his fellow diplomats—his fast friends united by a common homeland and a common love for this particular unknown—and look out of his twelfth-floor windows, alone, suspended, at peace, no Estela, no Sanjay, watching the sandstorm gather, the sudden sepia tone of his new city, his new northern capital.

Ash sat across from Leo in their first-class train car. He looked out the window at rows of cabbage and wheat, an empty condominium tower in the middle of a field, a man or woman in a wide-brimmed hat stabbing the earth near the tracks with a hoe, a low-rise concrete structure with a red cross painted on its roof. His phone was off and in his pocket. He'd invited Leo to play online Scrabble, which he knew Leo liked to do to improve his English vocabulary, but Leo had declined.

Ash had volunteered for the consular visit in Hebei a few weeks earlier, even though he'd overheard Leo—the locally engaged staffer who'd be accompanying him—call the assignment "a shit task in a shithole province" to one of the other Chinese embassy employees. Ash, who took every opportunity to leave Beijing and explore the country, had decided to go anyway.

It took four hours to reach the detention centre outside Shijiazhuang: thirty minutes from his apartment at Beijing's second ring road to the station, an hour and a half by high-speed train, and then a dusty and hot two hours in a rural cab, its vinyl seats covered with tasselled velvet. They slept overnight in a hotel and, the next morning, took another taxi to the facility gates. There, they were buzzed in through heavy metal doors flanked on either side by nine-foot fences topped with razor wire.

The detention centre, on the inside, looked more like an office. Its layout reminded Ash of his junior high school, with its long central corridor and several rooms coming off either side, though at the detention facility each doorway was gated with iron mesh and secured with a padlock. There was a large conference room at the end of the hall; through its open door Ash could see four or five oversized chairs around a boardroom table. Damian, the detainee, faced him as he approached.

There was another man in the room. He stood to greet Leo and Ash as they entered, then sat down again in the chair furthest from the door, in the corner. Two guards were also present, their batons jutting awkwardly from their hip holsters into their chair cushions. Ash sat across from Damian. Leo sat next to Ash, his notepad open on the table in front of him, ready to document.

"Est-ce qu'ils te traitent bien ici?" Ash asked.

Both the man and the detainee appeared startled. The man raised his hand in protest. Damian opened his mouth as if to answer, closed it, swallowed, and then spoke.

"Oui, assez bien," he replied.

"English only," the man said.

Ash smiled and relaxed into the plush chair. Damian smiled back.

"Who knew those public school French classes would pay off one day?" Damian said. "Hi. I'm Damian."

"Ash."

"Have you heard anything about my trial?"

"You cannot discuss the case," the man said in Mandarin. "Nor the trial."

"I don't know when the trial is," Ash said, responding to them both. Damian shuffled his feet under the table; Ash heard the clink of a chain and realized Damian's ankles were shackled. "You'll have to contact your lawyer for that."

"I know," Damian said. "Thought I'd ask, though. My family. Did they get my last letter?"

Ash pulled an envelope out of his back pocket. The man in the corner stood.

"I see that first," he said. Ash passed the letter to Leo, who leaned as far as he could over his right armrest to hand the envelope to the ministry official. The man used his fifth finger to tear open the sealed flap, then made a show of flipping through the pages. Finally, he folded the letter back into thirds and passed it back to Leo, who gave it to Ash, who gave it to Damian.

"It makes me want to cry, seeing this letter," Damian said, when he finished reading it. "And not just because of what's in it, or her handwriting. The letter itself. I know the kind of pen she used. I know the pages are torn from a Hilroy notebook, the kind we used in elementary school—probably our son's. I recognize your shirt. It's from the Gap, from a few years ago. I have the same one in a different colour."

Ash waited for him to continue. Damian had dark brown eyes and a long, narrow nose, a handsome face. He looked like someone Ash had known in junior high. He looked like someone he could have matched with on Tinder.

"I missed the last year of my son's life," Damian said, folding the pages and placing them on the table in front of him. The room was silent but for the thrum of the high-speed ceiling fan, which shook as it rotated.

"The Oilers," Damian said after a moment. "How are my Oilers?"

"Not doing as well as my Flames," Ash said.

Back at the hotel, Ash sat on the bed with his computer on his lap, his legs outstretched and his back against the wooden headboard. He connected to the hotel's Wi-Fi, then to his VPN, and then typed *Theodore MacPherson* into Google. He opened another tab and typed in *Theo MacPherson*—though his old schoolteacher didn't strike him as a Theo—and then a third tab with *Ted MacPherson*. After a few minutes of scrolling through the search results, some of which were purple from having been clicked on before, he shut his laptop and lay back on the bed.

He remembered walking down the hall in junior high, having been summoned out of science class. The first two knuckles of his right hand still throbbed. He'd won the previous day's fight with a single punch, a stab so fast and direct that the other boy, sitting up from where he'd landed on the pavement, had gotten to his feet, turned, and pushed through the crowd that had gathered without even looking back. The punch had been a shock to everyone but Ash, who'd been taking karate classes for years and had simply not told anyone.

He'd been in school with the other boy, Kevin, since kindergarten. The day before the fight, Ash had been walking home from the bus stop, Kevin and another eighth grader walking on the opposite side of the street, when he heard a shout.

"Hey, Paki!"

Ash kept walking.

"Hey. Paki!" Kevin and the other boy had stopped and turned to face him. Ash turned to them, perplexed.

"Yes?" Ash asked, uncertainly.

"Yes, you, dickhead," Kevin said.

Ash's cheeks reddened. He kept walking, more quickly now, and when he turned onto his street, he ran.

The next day at school, when Ash told Steven, who told Caleb, who told Kevin, that he would meet him in the yard near the baseball diamond at four, he did it not because he wanted to punch Kevin—in fact, the idea made him sick—but for his father, who looked as if *he'd* been punched, his face suddenly that of an old-looking Indian man as he said: *I moved halfway around the world, I redid all of my exams, I went through residency again, I pay for an expensive school, and my son still gets called Paki?*

And Ash, by the end of the whole episode, after his week-long detention—which, as it comprised doing his homework in the stillness of the old library, he quite enjoyed—never managed to actually ask anyone what the word *Paki* meant.

Worse than Kevin was the teacher who'd claimed to have broken up the fight, who'd brought an unwilling Kevin back into the ring and yelled at them both, though he'd looked only at Ash.

Ash later had him for English in ninth grade, and didn't get higher or lower than a B on any paper until he turned in a creative writing piece and received a C. There was never a single comment on any of his assignments, just the bright-red letter grade in the top right corner. When Mr. MacPherson found out that Ash had gotten 99 percent on the provincial exam, the highest mark in the class and one of the highest in the province, he'd said: *I'm surprised! Pleasantly, of course. I didn't know you had it in you.* When Ash was accepted into the writing program at an elite arts school for senior high, he'd said: *I'm amazed you got in. They've really lowered their standards, eh? Lucky for you!* It was one of Ash's biggest regrets that Mr. MacPherson had never known he'd gone to McGill, and then Columbia, and then into the diplomatic service, or that he'd had a poem published in the *Walrus*.

Thank God I had all of this other stuff going for me, Ash had told Estela once, *or a crappy teacher like that could have really changed my life for the worse. I still don't understand why he went out of his way to make me miserable.* Estela had said: *I know why. You were the only brown kid in your class, right? I know it's not always that, but sometimes it is. It happens all the time when we're together. I see it, you don't. You don't want to see it.*

The day following the consular visit, Ash texted Victor, the mayor's aide, whom he'd befriended over shots of baijiu the year before at a trade show. Ash invited him to lunch; Victor replied almost immediately and suggested a noodle shop near City Hall.

They met in front of the restaurant, and a waitress led them to a shaded table outside. It was a hot day, and Victor was wearing a long-sleeved white shirt, the underarms and back of which were soaked in sweat.

"Long time no see," Victor said as he sat down. "I'm happy to see you again."

"Me too," Ash said. Victor ordered two Tsingtao beers and two bottles of water as Ash flipped through the menu. *Rural old meat*, he read, in English, beneath a picture of a fried chicken dish. The Chinese description was more appealing: *Country-style traditional chicken in a soy, hoisin, and chili pepper sauce*. "I might get this."

"I've had it before. It's good. I'll get the same thing but with rice," Victor said.

The drinks came out quickly. While they waited for their food, Ash asked Victor about his girlfriend and new cat, both of whom figured prominently in his WeChat Moments. Victor asked if Ash had had any success on Tantan, a Chinese dating app, which Ash had forgotten he'd complained to Victor about.

After a few moments of companionable silence, Victor placed his hands, palms down, on the table.

"Can I ask you something? I'm not sure if anything can be done, but of everyone I know, you might be able to do something."

Ash looked up in surprise. "Sure, go ahead. Anything I can do."

Victor leaned over the table, lowering his voice and switching to English.

"My boss, the mayor," he said. "He doesn't like to talk about it, but his daughter is at McGill. He recognized your McGill tie the last time you were here. He's wondering if you can help her. He says that if you can help her, he can help you."

Victor paused.

"His daughter is being harassed. By her boyfriend, a rich kid from Shanghai, also in his first year, the son of an executive at Dongfeng Motor. He tells her what to wear, takes her cellphone. Siwen called her father from a friend's phone to say he'd threatened her, that he'd said he didn't know what he'd do if he came back and she wasn't in his room where he'd left her."

Their food arrived, and Victor fell silent. "That's not the worst part," he continued, as the waitress moved back toward the kitchen. "She's started cutting her arms again, and even when she does have her phone, she's stopped taking her father's calls. He's very worried and there is nothing he can do. To intervene at a high level would expose the fact that she's there, which would expose him here. And he doesn't want to get on the wrong side of Dongfeng, as they employ a lot of people in Shijiazhuang."

A group of four men at a nearby table laughed loudly. Victor flinched. He finished his beer in two quick gulps, stabbed at his chicken and rice with his chopsticks, and continued.

"Is there anything you can do? You know how things work at McGill. Maybe you still know someone there. He has drugs in his dorm room. In his bottom drawer, in a box he uses for petty cash as the treasurer of the students' society. Siwen found it."

For a minute, neither spoke. Ash heard a clatter of dishes in the kitchen, the smash of a glass, and the sound of a faraway, high-pitched siren moving closer. He ate a few bites of chicken, twisting the slippery noodles around his chopsticks. A cyclist sped by, his rear basket overburdened with oranges.

"That's terrible. I'm so sorry about his daughter," Ash said finally. "I'll think about what I can do. Nothing comes to mind," he added quickly. "Also..." He paused. "You and I are friends, but how do I know this is true? I don't want to help put an innocent kid behind bars."

"You don't," Victor said. "But if they search his room and he doesn't have drugs, there's no harm done, right?"

"Fair enough."

"Please do consider it." Victor relaxed his grip on the table slats and motioned to the waitress for another beer. "It's like working for an ogre. He shuts himself in his office and jumps out and yells at me for the slightest mistake."

"I'm really impressed you know the word *ogre* in English," Ash said.

As they were leaving—Victor had been more relaxed through the second half of lunch, ordering a third, and then a fourth, beer—Ash said, "I almost forgot. You said the mayor could help me. Help me with what?"

"Your prisoner," Victor said. "He knows the business owner who originally pushed the police to lay charges. He says he can get those dropped."

Ash met Ophélie the summer he turned thirty-four, the year after he returned from Beijing. He'd taken an assignment in Montreal, at the department of Global Affairs' regional office, ostensibly to work closely with the video game industry but more truly because he missed the city and Nik was there. He rented the top floor of a duplex in the Plateau, a stone's throw from where he'd lived over a decade earlier as a student.

He'd been biking west on Rachel, turning south onto Mentana. Ophélie had been driving the oncoming car and Ash had been certain that she'd seen him, his arm extended, signalling his left turn. Ash, after all, had seen Ophélie, her hands high on the steering wheel, her gaze focused ahead. He'd even managed to notice, before the front wheel of her SUV clipped his back one and he crashed onto the road, his bike landing on top of him, how pretty she was.

Ophélie stopped the car in the middle of the intersection. Ash was sitting up, and Ophélie had one of his hands in hers, saying something. Through the ringing in his ears, Ash thought he heard her apologize. Ophélie had taken a few two-by-twos of gauze from the side pocket of her scrub pants and was pressing them into his palm. It was then that Ash realized he was bleeding.

Fifteen minutes later, he was in the passenger seat of her car, his left hand applying pressure to the palm of his right, as Ophélie walked out of the bicycle repair shop on the corner.

"Well, they basically hate me for hitting a cyclist, but they said they'd fix your bike for free."

Ash nodded, still disoriented.

"I am so, so sorry, again," Ophélie said. "How's your hip? I took a quick look when you were on the road and I don't think anything is broken. No laceration there either."

Twenty minutes later they pulled into the parking lot of the Royal Victoria Hospital. Ash still hadn't managed to say anything. His right thigh was throbbing. He held a fistful of blood-darkened gauze in his right hand. He was still unsure how badly he'd been cut.

"I thought you left an hour ago," the triage nurse said as they walked in.

"Yeah, not good news, I'm afraid," Ophélie said. "I hit this guy on my drive home. My fault. Car versus bike."

After six hours in the ER, Ash emerged with ten stitches in his right palm, vaguely in the shape of a lightning bolt. It was dark by the time he and Ophélie returned to the bike shop, collapsed the back seats, and put his bicycle in the back of her SUV. She insisted on driving him home.

Before he got out of the car at the corner of Rachel and de la Roche, Ophélie asked Ash for his insurance information. He asked her for her phone number.

What Ash loved about Ophélie, even that first day: not only that she'd brought him to the ER and waited with him to be stitched up, when she could have just called him an ambulance, but that she'd taken him to *her* ER and borne the questions and critical looks of her colleagues, who were familiar with the potential consequences of working a twelve-hour overnight shift and then driving home, but who still, Ash could tell, thought a bit less of her for having hit him.

In the mornings, waking beside her, the windows open and the white linen curtains billowing inward, she would hold his damaged right palm with its cicatricial lightning bolt and kiss it, in zigzag, and say, *Oh, beautiful day*, and he would never know if she meant this one or that first one.

Early one October morning three years later, single again, an email from Estela arrived in his inbox. At first he thought it was junk; the subject line was empty, and the body of the message seemed to contain just a link until he saw, underneath, *Thought you would like this!* followed by her email signature.

Ash clicked on the link, which took him to a website with photos of hundreds of bookshelves: in people's homes, at used bookstores and libraries, in burned-out ruins and war zones, on bedside tables.

You're right, I LOVED that. How are you? he typed in reply, and then, not waiting even a moment—though the email had been sent at 8:17 and it was now 8:26—he hit Send.

Ash was in the middle of a second date with a woman he'd met on Hinge when Estela called in early spring, five months after she'd reconnected by email. He looked at his phone, which was face down on the table beside his knife, with surprise.

"I'm sorry, I thought the ringer was off," he said. It was, but when he turned the phone over and saw the caller's name, he realized what had happened; he'd put Estela, years ago, along with his father, mother, and brother, on his emergency bypass list.

"I think this is an emergency. I have to take this," Ash said, standing, leaving his jacket on the back of his chair and walking out of the restaurant and onto the sidewalk. He could see his date through the window, looking down at her phone.

"Estela?" he said.

"A blast from the past, right?"

Ten minutes later, Ash went back in and sat across from his date.

"I'm so sorry about that," he said. "A friend in crisis."

Ash's corn chowder had cooled, but he ate what was left of it in quick spoonfuls.

"How was the skate?" he asked, noticing that her plate was empty.

"It was great," she replied. "So, how long have you been on Hinge? I forgot to ask last time."

"You were my first Hinge date," Ash said.

"Wow, really?"

Ash leaned back in his chair and smiled. Estela, in town for the weekend, had asked if he could meet her at their old café in an hour, and in his mind he was already walking up Saint-Denis, on his way to her. "How has it been going for you?" he asked.

"Well, I'm still going on second dates," she said, and laughed.

"How was your date?" Estela asked. She sat in a refurbished pew, next to a couple playing chess. Ash removed his toque and set it on the table momentarily before taking the seat across from her.

"It was fine," Ash replied. "It's so nice to see you."

"Fourteen years, right?" Estela said. Her face had softened, but the sharp cheekbones were the same. Her bright regard out to the world was the same. She was still beautiful.

"I'm really sorry about the morning I ran off on you," Estela said. "I'd never told anyone about Ethan and I was horrified that I had. Horrified it would be something you'd refer to, and that we'd have to talk about, from then on."

"I—"

"Hold on," she interrupted. She smiled in apology. "And then, many therapy sessions later—I've been in therapy since Allister and I broke up in June—I realized that I'd told you because I was comfortable telling you, and because I wanted to tell someone. But then I worried that too much time had passed. That the path between you and me had overgrown, so to speak."

Ash let her continue.

"Anyway. I'm also sorry for the day I saw you through the bus window and pretended I didn't."

"That's okay," Ash said. "It's forgiven. I missed you, but it's forgiven."

"How was Ottawa, in the end?" Estela asked, as a server placed a bowl of chicken and couscous between them. She spooned braised carrots and potatoes onto her plate, motioning to the bowl with her free hand.

"Oh, no thanks," Ash said. "I liked Ottawa. I know it's anathema to you to say that."

"I came around to Ottawa during law school," Estela said. "It turns out I only hated it the way any adventuring soul hates the place they grew up. Besides, it was nice to have those years near my parents."

"How are your parents?" Ash asked, keeping his voice light.

"The same," Estela said. "They've been the same since 1994. They still do stuff. They have friends over, they do board-game nights. My dad plays golf. My mom goes for walks with their dog in Gatineau Park."

The waiter returned with mint tea and sugar served in a ceramic dish shaped like a tagine. Estela paused while the waiter poured the tea.

"They have enough photos and videos of Ethan's seven-year life to fill the next twenty of theirs," Estela continued. "I was home last weekend. Everything's been digitized. They have a Google Photos account with just his photos in it."

Estela added a spoonful of sugar to her tea, took a sip, and asked about Ophélie. Ash described the mangalsutra with the gold leaf-shaped pendant he'd planned to present to her along with the engagement ring, and then added on the story of Andrés, after which Estela joined him on his side of the table, gleefully sending taps to potential male matches on Grindr. After a few minutes of this—Estela had selected four or five beefy gym types shaped like inverted triangles, all of whom worked as strippers—she stacked his clean plate below hers and mimed the dimensions and handle of a to-go box to the server.

"I'm guessing you don't want this?" Estela asked.

"No, I had a huge lunch," Ash said. "Still a food scavenger, I see."

"Yes," she said, laughing. "Not so much during the time I was with Allister, as he loved to cook, but now again, certainly, yes."

The server brought a box and Estela scooped the remaining half-portion into it.

Ash cleared his throat as Estela stood to put on her coat. "The letter to the university," he said. "You haven't told me what you want me to say in it."

Estela looked into the middle distance, pulling her arm through her coat sleeve. "Oh, you know. Just what you saw happen. That he was my prof. That we were sleeping together. Mention the letter he wrote for me for U of T."

"That's it?"

"That's it," she said.

Outside the café, a sharp breeze lifted the edges of Ash's scarf. He kept his hands in his pockets to guard against the cold.

Estela said, "I looked at the photos when I was home. It made me sad to see them. Not sad to see him, at least not any more than it usually does. What's sad is how old and grainy the photos are. How long ago it was. His little nineties-style shorts."

The March wind tunnelled down the street in long gusts. Estela turned to face Ash. Her hat covered her hair and ears, making her face, blanched already from the cold, seem even more exposed. Ash reached a hand to her shoulder, pulling her closer, wrapping his other arm around her back. She rested her head against his collarbone, her breath against his neck. Then she pulled away, holding his bare hand in her mittened one for a few seconds before taking a step back. Then they set out together, heading east on Mont-Royal.

"You know, it's funny—and this is more stuff that's come out in therapy—but in my twenties, and even through most of my thirties, I desperately wanted to have a baby," Estela continued. "I felt like it was my fault we'd lost Ethan, that if I'd been babysitting instead it wouldn't have happened. And since I couldn't take that back, I could at least give my parents a grandchild, another little boy, to love. I know it doesn't really make sense."

They detoured onto the street for a moment to accommodate a woman with a double stroller.

"Anyway, it took me most of these last nine months to understand that Ethan's death wasn't on me, that I was placing too much of a burden on myself. And that even if I managed to alleviate their loss with a grandchild, which is unlikely, it wouldn't change mine. I was finally able to separate the loss of my brother from the loss of their son, and feel like my grief, while lesser, was legitimate."

"I don't know that it was lesser," Ash said.

Estela turned to him and shrugged as if to say, *Who knows?* She took a step into the crosswalk on Rivard, then stopped for the light. "Their shrine—because that's what it is, his room laid out exactly as it was, down to his framed school photos and peeling *Lion King* poster—I know it's not good. They've never recovered. I don't think they ever seriously tried."

Ash and Estela crossed the street together and continued toward the Metro station, following a path recently cleared of snow.

"I'm not saying I would have done any better. Allister certainly didn't," Estela said. "But it made me realize that I do want a child. Not to replace my parents' son, not to replace my brother, but to have that kind of weight in my life, for better or for worse. And that even if I didn't state the reason perfectly at the time, I'd given Allister the right answer."

Estela's eyes rested on Ash's for a second. "See you soon?"

"Sooner than fourteen years, I hope," he said.

Estela hugged him and turned, her tall green rucksack the last part of her he saw as she descended the escalator into the station.

It was a bright September day six months after his reunion with Estela. Ash had gone to his gym—on Saint-André, in the Gay Village—over his lunch break. There, he'd noticed a cute guy using one of the squat racks, with three forty-five-pound plates on either side of the bar. Ash watched his slim, strong shoulders tighten as he bent at the knees, the curve of the tip of his penis perceptible through his maroon gym shorts as he sat on a bench between sets. Afterwards, Ash had stopped for a sandwich on Sainte-Catherine and seen him again.

"Hey," Ash said.

The young man looked up from his tablet.

"We go to the same gym," Ash said. "Your squat is impressive."

"Hey, thanks," he said. He moved his empty sandwich wrapper back onto his side of the table. "I'm Alex. Want to sit?"

They sat at Subway for two hours—ordering another half-sandwich to share when the lone employee started to glare at them—their fifteen-year age gap disappearing as they talked.

"My dad, I think, knows I'm gay," Alex said. "My mom guessed a few years ago and asked me directly. I think she was excited to have a gay son. It allowed her to show her friends how woke she was." He laughed. "I'm kidding. My mom is really nice. Really supportive."

"I told my parents much later," Ash said. "I'm bi, actually. I think I started to realize it—well, this is going to be completely meaningless to you since you're twenty-two, but there was a band in the late nineties called the Backstreet Boys. And one of the members, the tall, lanky, blond one, was exactly my type. I honestly liked their music, too," he said. "I've never admitted that last part to anyone."

They laughed. Ash moved his deadlift-shoed toe a few inches forward to touch Alex's. Alex moved his fingers forward slightly, reaching a bit more than halfway across the table, but without making contact with Ash's.

"My parents were really good about it," Ash continued. "Growing up, they were your typical strict Indian parents. But they adapted. I mean, they were overjoyed a couple of years ago when I said I was going to propose to my then girlfriend, and I think they'd still prefer it if I married a woman. But if I brought a nice man home, I think they'd adjust."

Ash crumpled the sandwich wrapper in his fist, stuffed it into its accompanying plastic bag, then continued. "I think they're more afraid I'm going to meet someone overseas on posting and just stay there. It's hard to date—especially here, back home," he said. He looked down at the table. "It's hard to find someone who's willing to move every few years and have their career always come second."

"I love the idea of living abroad," Alex said.

Ash looked up at Alex. "Like my next posting," he said. "Three years in Albania."

SASHA

Sasha was already in his cycling gear and on his way out when he saw the browser tab on his husband's computer. He'd gone into their study to check the Weather Channel—to see if he'd need his winter helmet, the one with the insulated liner and earflaps—and had sat in the wheeled office chair, logged in to the desktop, and opened a new browser tab.

It was four degrees. Insulated helmet, then. As he stood, he caught sight of one of the other open tabs: *LGBT Adoption in 2021*. And then the ones beside it, all with similar subjects: *Coalition des familles LGBT, Adopting a Child in Quebec, Same Sex Adoption*.

Sasha's hand rested motionless on the mouse, which sat on a pad that resembled a miniature oriental carpet. Then he left the room, grabbed his helmet from the winter-gear drawer at the front entrance, and got on his bike.

All through the twenty-minute ride to Concordia—Sasha was doing his master's degree and had an early-morning class—he thought, *I was just checking the weather. To know what helmet to use. And your desktop was closer.*

He repeated this to himself, over and over—because it was true, but also as if practising, in case he were asked later, in a fit of righteous anger, in a court of law, exactly what he'd been doing snooping on his husband's computer.

Though, as it turned out, he was never asked. And then, as the days went by, and there was no mention of adoption, of having children, of hiring a surrogate, of even a desire to have a baby, Sasha began to feel indignant himself.

And so the next time his husband left—for a gym class he'd signed up for pre-pandemic that was now in-person again—Sasha sat down at his husband's computer, this time intentionally, and opened his browser history. Pornhub.com, from last night: fine. Often they watched together. *Fifty-Two Gift Ideas for Your Husband*, which he clicked past quickly, in case it would ruin a surprise. And then the list of adoption agencies, which he'd already seen.

Sasha moved over to his husband's email account and searched for the name of one of the agencies. There were a dozen or so newsletters dating back to November 2020, and a draft email, which contained a half-completed application form.

Before he could stop himself, he then searched for his partner's ex by name. There was an entire page of results with his ex's name in the subject field, but which his husband had composed and then sent to himself. Sasha, again unable to resist, clicked on the most recent one, from October 2018: *There are two things to repeat to yourself when your beloved's shadow follows and then fades out behind you. Confident in your steps, you can tell yourself: if not love, then a delicate unknown tomorrow. Then, as the bright sun forces you to shield your eyes, as your outline alone becomes marked against the harsh sidewalk, you will think: there is no water beyond you, only thirst.*

The next week they flew out west, where Sasha's mother-in-law was in the ICU. From her hospital room Sasha could see mountain peaks in the distance, their tops obscured in cloud, and the city itself, which seemed interminable. He'd been left alone with her while his husband went to get coffee. She rested a few feet away, in a raised bed bathed in fading daylight, the only sounds the mechanical intake and exhale of the ventilator.

Sasha had met his mother-in-law two years ago. He'd been invited for Thanksgiving, and even though the trip was to take place only six weeks after he and his partner had met, and he'd been asked to go after a mere three weeks of dating, he'd said yes, against the advice of his friends and family, who'd thought they were moving too fast. She'd made roast beef, Yorkshire pudding, shepherd's pie, and beef stew, joking that she'd only learned to cook once she'd moved to England. His partner's parents lived on a lake, and the four of them would sit on the dock, under heated lamps, talking until midnight. Sasha remembered that he'd admired his now husband, so comfortable in his gay skin, holding Sasha's hand in restaurants, leaning in close on a crowded bus and nuzzling his neck with his nose and his rough, bearded chin.

And now his mother-in-law was in the ICU with COVID-19. Unfairly: a seventy-year-old internist close to retirement, she'd heeded the call from her overrun former hospital and helped to man the COVID-19 ward just down the hall from where she now lay. She'd had two doses of the vaccine and had still ended up here, with sky-high phosphate and uric acid levels; wondering why, her doctors had done a whole-body CT and found the tumour lodged next to her spine.

His husband was still downstairs—he'd just texted, *There's no milk, do you want cream?*—when Sasha heard a prolonged beep from the monitor, then the sound of many bodies running down the hall, pausing at the door to don PPE. And then the voice overhead: *Code Blue, sixth floor, ICU.*

Sasha watched his partner—now back in the home he'd grown up in, his palms face up in his lap as he sat in silence, looking out at the placid lake—while his father-in-law prepared soup. The slow, methodical chop of a chef's knife was audible from the kitchen.

"I barely knew my mother," his husband finally said. "I found out just last year that they'd wanted a third child but had trouble conceiving. And giving up physics to go into medicine—did she ever regret that?"

He raised his hands slightly, just above his knees, as if asking the question with them, as if asking, *What else does this universe hold?*

"My grandparents lived so far away and died when I was really young. I don't even know their names. We had to draw a family tree in Grade 6 and mine was abysmal."

He stood and began pacing in front of the floor-to-ceiling windows that looked out onto the lake.

"There was a weekend," he continued, "a few years ago now. Mom was coming to Montreal to visit me. And I had the choice of picking up some overtime at work. I felt bad doing it, since I only saw her a few times a year, but I did. To be honest, the idea of spending forty-eight hours with her, just one-on-one, made me nervous. I never knew what to say."

He turned to face Sasha. From where Sasha sat, his partner was backlit, the nearly setting sun behind him, the partly frozen lake and the surrounding light giving the snow a light blue hue.

"I had only twenty-five days with her after that. I counted, in the middle of the night, last night. And now, all I can think is that I could have had twenty-six."

On their way back to Montreal, seated over the wing, travelling through dense grey cloud, Sasha asked, "I know we haven't talked about it since our second date, but where are you now, in terms of having kids?"

OPHÉLIE

On that midsummer Thursday—on what became the worst day of Ophélie's life—Ash had been in Italy for his brother's bachelor party, and Ophélie wondered, months later, if his absence then had primed her to walk out the weekend of his next boys' trip, to Mont-Tremblant, on New Year's Eve. As if the decision to leave had been prompted by the symmetry of it. As if the July absence that, to her, had signalled a betrayal, once repeated, in December, could only signal another betrayal.

Not that, Ophélie knew, what had happened that Thursday was anyone's fault but hers. Or even hers, as the hospital quality-improvement committee eventually determined. The report had used the terms *Swiss-cheese model, institutional flaw, unlikely individual error*. Still, despite her formal exoneration, for months Ophélie tiptoed through the hospital as if walking barefoot over shattered glass, as if there'd be another emergency—another crashing child—around the next corner, during the next minute, of her shift.

On the ward the Tuesday after the incident, Ash still in Italy, Ophélie noticed a chart with a raised yellow tab and retrieved it from the cart, turning to the flagged Orders section. But when she saw the prescription, she flipped past it—her heart pounding, staring unseeingly at the page of vital signs she'd landed on instead—and then closed the chart, leaving the epinephrine prescription for another nurse to verify, tear out, and send down to the hospital's pharmacy.

At a party the weekend after that, Ophélie wasn't even able to answer when a stranger asked her what she did. "She's a nurse," Ash finally replied for her, squeezing her hand, worried.

At the very second of her mistake, as she'd injected the medication into the child's vein instead of her muscle, Ash had been in Pisa, near the tower, the photo he'd texted her at that instant making it seem as if he were pushing back against the leaning structure, a touristy pose he knew she would hate.

Ophélie had called in sick the day after the incident and was in bed when she got the text from Anca, her best friend from nursing school, who worked in the ICU at the Montreal Children's Hospital. *Thought you'd want an update on your kid,* Anca wrote. *Dr. Freeman is worried about the long-term effects on the heart, but she's fine otherwise. She's sitting up in bed and making charm bracelets for everyone.*

Ophélie got up and carried the congealed bowl of ramen she'd ordered in for lunch over to the sink. She felt sick. A drone filled her ears. Her vision was blurred, the objects around her bright in the afternoon sunlight. She realized she was crying.

She looked up the girl's results on her computer. Troponin levels—which Ophélie had only ever seen ordered for adults who'd had heart attacks—had been drawn twice in the last twelve hours and were elevated, but trending down. Everything else was normal. Ophélie read the patient's most recent nursing note and saw that she was being transferred back to the ward later that day. She exhaled. She briefly closed her eyes.

She moved over to the couch and scrolled through the text messages on her phone. Ash had written, *You okay?* twelve hours after having sent the photo. Ophélie still hadn't texted back.

When, a few hours later, having taken a shower and loaded the contents of the sink into the dishwasher, Ophélie finally replied, *Something awful happened*, Ash called right away and offered to fly home. He was angry—his breath coming in short bursts as he walked around the piazza, trying to find a quiet spot—that, of the dozen or so individuals in the room at the time, the blame had fallen squarely on her.

"Where was the doctor in all of this?" he asked.

"There were several," she replied. "Residents, the attending from the ward, an ICU staff."

"And nobody said anything? When you said you were going to do the injection via the IV?"

"Maybe they didn't hear me," Ophélie said.

Ophélie tried to clarify to the committee, but also to herself, what had happened. "The most I can say," she said to the packed boardroom, "is that in the confusion of the ICU team arriving, and Inma struggling to get the line in, and the mother asking over and over what was happening, and the beep of the heart rate monitor going what I knew was now over one hundred—all I could think, and what the order for epinephrine confirmed, was that this was an emergency. And in an emergency you need an IV, which is why were we waiting for Inma to get one. Therefore the epinephrine was meant to go IV. And I said, out loud, 'Epinephrine 0.5 milligrams IV push,' as I was giving it, and nobody said anything."

A resident sitting across from her said, "I heard you. And I thought, that doesn't sound right, for anaphylaxis. But nobody else said anything, including the ICU staff who was there, so I figured I was wrong about what I'd thought was right."

Over the following weeks, Ophélie would dream that she'd stopped herself.

She was at the patient's bedside but the clock was broken, its second hand ticking in place, back and forth, over the four. When she placed the needle into the hub of the IV tube, the resident who'd spoken up in the committee meeting jumped to her feet—wearing a crown, which Ophélie recognized from a board game she'd played as a child, and carrying a sword, which resembled Sailor Moon's—climbed onto a chair, and yelled, *Stop!* The resident waved a black-and-white-checkered Formula 1 flag in wide arcs over the patient, whose face was as smooth and featureless as a mannequin's.

In the dream, she'd put down the syringe, the clock ticked past the four and on toward the five, and the patient turned to her, with her restored, ruddy, adolescent face.

And yet for months and years thereafter, another dream, this one unresolved: the patient drowning, first reaching one hand out of the water and then the other, then ever so briefly her head, and Ophélie with the life-saving buoy, which she attempted to throw over and over again, only to have it stick to her hands.

When Ash returned from Italy exactly one week after the incident, he brought Ophélie a pendant: a delicate glass fish in a delicate glass fishbowl, a gift from Venice. His first night back, he drew her a bath and cooked her dinner. He let Ophélie be speechless. He let her lie in bed until ten in the morning. He paid her credit card bill and her electricity bill out of his own pocket when he saw them on the counter and realized they were overdue. He slept at her place, rubbing her back at night until she fell asleep.

Ophélie knew it wasn't Ash's fault. But his not being there had made her feel alone, with him, in her relationship with him, for the first time—when she'd thought she'd never feel that way again.

It brought back Étienne and every moment of the two years they'd been together. It brought back being eight years old, the day her mother had blamed her for knocking over the pot of basil on the counter when she hadn't, when it had been placed near the edge and had fallen over on its own, and Ophélie had run away—down the street, for mere minutes, but with a loneliness borne of the injustice that felt interminable.

And so, perhaps, it was the remembered aloneness—the pot of basil, Étienne, Italy—all accumulated, that second boys' weekend, that made Ophélie walk away.

Ophélie's relationship with Étienne began on Saint-Jean-Baptiste Day, the summer she turned seventeen. They were sitting around the bonfire on the public beach, he across from her, his eye caught by her blue-and-white bikini. He'd walked a full semicircle around the fire, smoke in his eyes, to lean a hand over her shoulder and offer her a can of Molson Dry. Ophélie, whenever Étienne retold this story, didn't have the heart to tell him that the swimsuit wasn't hers, that she'd found it in the closet of the cottage they always rented for the summer.

Étienne was her first kiss. He was also the first boy she ever had sex with, though she'd waited until the end of their first summer together for that. They'd walked the length of the private beach behind Étoile's camp cabins until they arrived at the enclosure they'd scoped out the day before, bounded on one side by a boulder and on the other by the drooping branch of a leafy tree. Ophélie had lain on a bed of red and gold leaves, their maple-leaf imprint on her back and then her chest, her hip bones pressed into the hardened sand.

Ophélie's parents, both teachers, had the summers off and always spent July and August in the Laurentians. When Ophélie was younger, she went to Étoile, the nearby summer camp, on weekdays. As a teenager, she spent days reading in the hammock her father strung up between the oak trees near the lake, or sunbathing at the public beach—a ten-minute canoe trip away—with her former camp friends.

One year, when they were both twelve, Étienne was at camp with her. He teased her about her long legs—legs that a few years later he would caress with his tongue, tracing the backs of her knees—and nicknamed her Tipule, after the leggy insect. At the end of that summer he'd handed her a rose under the dense cover of trees, then turned and walked back to the bunks, leaving her alone in the forest holding the single stem, jagged with thorns.

During their early teens, after that, their paths didn't cross—though Ophélie would often watch him, at a distance, sometimes playing hacky sack with friends but more often alone, wandering by the shore and kicking pebbles, hands in his pockets, gaze set downward.

Étienne never mentioned the rose. He in fact pretended, to her and to others, perhaps even to himself, that he'd never seen her crane-fly legs before that Saint-Jean-Baptiste Day, clad in her fleur-de-lys top and bottoms.

It was largely thanks to that bathing suit that Étienne expected the conversation to go better than it did when he gifted her a copy of *Les boeufs sont lents mais la terre est patiente* for her seventeenth birthday. They'd started that July—a week after having reconnected at the bonfire—as camp counsellors at Étoile, Ophélie in charge of the twelve-year-old girls and Étienne in charge of the thirteen-year-old boys. They met up in the evenings in the padlocked lacrosse equipment shed to chat and cuddle; to this end, Étienne had repurposed a mattress from a boys' cabin after one of the nine-year-olds had been airlifted out with a femur fracture.

"We're two minutes into your birthday," he said, kissing her cheek and then handing her the book, with its sepia-toned cover and portrait of Pierre Falardeau.

"Thank you," Ophélie said, obviously unsure of what it was she was holding.

"You don't recognize it?"

"I know who it is," she replied.

"For me, this is the work, *the work*, of the Quebec sovereignty movement," he said.

Ophélie dropped his hand. "I didn't know you were souverainiste," she said.

"Of course I am. Every Québécois is, once they really think about it. As soon as they realize the union with Ottawa is just historical circumstance, not the way things have to be."

"I don't know that I am," Ophélie said. "I don't know that I'm not, but I don't know that I am."

"Read this book and you will be," Étienne said.

Years later, sitting on the couch with Ash, having just watched the Flames beat the Jets and not having heard Étienne's name for nearly a decade, his face, that small scar on his right cheek, appeared on the screen before them.

"Oh, God," Ophélie said.

"What?"

She paused. "I used to date that guy."

"Really? That guy?" Ash asked. "He's running for the Liberal party?"

"I guess so," Ophélie said. "Which is funny, because he used to be a diehard separatist."

Ophélie remembered her last conversation with Étienne—after he'd told her he was opening a motorcycle shop and asked her to move in with him, and Ophélie had responded that she was moving to Montreal to become a nurse—when he'd said, *Fine, go and live with the anglos*, and she'd said, *You're living an old dream*, to which he'd shouted, *You say that because you have no soul*, and she had shouted, *You say that because you have no brain.*

She remembered the weekend Étienne had gotten that scar, the summer she'd turned eighteen. She'd convinced her mother to let her go canoe camping with him—a tough sell given her mother had disliked Étienne from the start—and the two of them had set off on a cloudless Saturday.

Ophélie was an able, even expert, canoeist, but where the Rivière Rouge turned rough she was in the bow, Étienne in the stern, and she could do little to evade the rapids and then the rocks. The canoe capsized, the blade of Étienne's paddle snapping against the shallow river bottom, then popping up from below and slashing his cheek.

They'd both ended up on the shore, their canoe lodged in a net of branches just downstream but unreachable, a paddle and a half between them, with no cellphones and a looming, hot two-hour trek back.

It was why Ophélie was all the more surprised when, sitting beside her on a rock, his left hand cupping his bleeding right cheek, Étienne chose this moment to say, "I hate those fucking shorts."

"What?"

"I hate those fucking shorts. They're indecent."

Ophélie, too taken aback to speak, watched the red droplets form between his fingers and drip onto the grey-brown clay of the exposed riverbed.

"How are they indecent?"

"They are too short." He enunciated each word clearly, slowly, as if she were half-deaf.

"For whom?" she asked, bewildered.

"For me. Definitely not too short for any other man who would look at them, though. Clearly that's intentional on your part."

They sat in silence for a few minutes. The bleeding stopped; Étienne wiped his bloodied left hand against his wet pant leg.

Ophélie stared out over the water. But Étienne wasn't done yet.

"Like, what is this?" he said, hooking his thumb and forefinger around the hem of her jean shorts, pulling the denim an inch or two away from her leg and then letting the fabric go. "How can you be mine if every man can see you like this?"

This was an old fight. The last time, they'd been on a deserted playground, a rusty merry-go-round turning behind them, his index finger pulling down the V of her tank top, nearly exposing her breasts. He'd released his finger and said, *Do you wear this kind of trashy stuff so other men will look at you?* and then hopped back on the squealing carousel, not waiting for a reply, kicking himself forward with his feet.

This time, she wanted to say, *I don't fucking belong to you*, but instead continued to sit quietly, fingering the splintered edge of the broken paddle as the sun passed its midpoint, sending its rays across the glittering water.

The wound—likely owing to the tiny slivers of wood that had remained embedded in Étienne's cheek—healed poorly over the following weeks. It meant that Ophélie avoided looking at his face during his next outburst, an unfortunate circumstance that likely made the onslaught worse.

"I don't see that it's unfair," Étienne said, holding her hand as they walked down the boardwalk at the public beach, a few steps behind a group of their friends.

"How is it not? You can go skinny-dipping and I can't? I don't want or need to, but that's not the point."

"It's fair because you don't care if I go skinny-dipping, so my going skinny-dipping does you no harm. I care if you go skinny-dipping, because I love you enough to not want other men to see you naked, so you going skinny-dipping does me harm. Therefore I should be allowed to go, and you not."

Étienne momentarily released her hand to readjust his backpack.

"Don't get me wrong," he continued. "I don't want or need to either, but it's the principle."

Ophélie, emboldened by the presence of their friends nearby, then said, "Do you care if another woman sees me naked?"

In response Étienne dropped her hand, strode ahead, and spent the rest of the afternoon walking five paces in front of her, his head bent in fury, at that angle Ophélie had come to know so well.

Étienne could be tender, too, loving to the point of self-effacement—like the night he told Ophélie that she was the only good thing in his life, that he was afraid she'd leave like his father had left. That he'd had a dream that she'd left him, and when he'd awoken he'd wanted to walk down into the deepest part of the Rivière Rouge and allow himself to be swept away, water and crustaceans crowding his throat, his eyes red, his body curved into the gentle form of a C as he was dragged along, drowning, down to the Saint Lawrence River.

Their second-last fight occurred at the beginning of their third—and final—summer together, when Maxime, an architecture student and a friend of Étienne's brother, Guillaume, came to visit for the weekend. Maxime, who rowed for UdeM, had spent most of that Friday evening on Guillaume's swivel chair playing *World of Warcraft*, shirtless.

And yes, Ophélie had been staring at him.

Étienne waited two days to bring it up. He waited, in fact, until her parents were back in Quebec City for a weekend, until her cellphone was in the next room. For a brief second, and then again later, Ophélie wondered if he'd done that on purpose.

"What was the other day about?"

Étienne sat on the edge of her bed, opposite her, his voice soft.

"What do you mean?" Ophélie asked, turning to face her vanity table, even though she knew exactly what he meant. She busied her hands with her eyeshadow palettes, stacking them into towers.

"With Max-ime," he said in singsong, as if the name had two parts. Her back to him, Ophélie could still see half of his face, as well as his torso, reflected in the antique mirror that hung on the wall. Étienne was smiling a tight, clown-like smile. He gripped the duvet so tightly Ophélie could see the veins on the backs of his hands.

"I don't know what you mean." Ophélie knocked over a bottle of nail polish, which skittered across the dressing table and fell with a soft thud onto the carpeted floor.

Étienne stood and moved toward her. He put his hand against the back of her neck, his thumb on one side and his forefinger on the other, at first gently, then with increasing pressure. Ophélie saw, in a flash, an image of him throwing her head forward into the mirror, the crack in the glass, the blood on her forehead.

Instead, he let go.

"Don't you ever embarrass me like that again. Acting like a slut."

Maybe I am a slut, Ophélie thought. *Because you're right, I did want to fuck him.*

Ophélie maintained—both to herself and then to her mother, who'd asked her point-blank the afternoon she'd walked into Ophélie's room to drop off clean laundry and found her daughter curled up in bed, crying—that Étienne had never raped her. And, in truth, he hadn't.

He did, however, ensure all fights ceased immediately when sex was offered or agreed to. Sex was also the only way he could be convinced that, yes, she loved him, too. And he never stopped to consider if the sex he sought—and received her hollow, flat consent to—would make her wet enough to give her pleasure, as long as she was wet enough to give him pleasure.

All of which meant that, years later, the touch of a desired stranger's hand could leave her as dry as winter's bark, and as afraid of her body's reaction to the possibility of sex—*Would those inner folds become, again, like sandpaper? Would he notice?*—as she was of sex itself.

Ophélie never told him, but the second person she'd ever had sex with was Ash, after over a decade of complete celibacy, of inviting dates up to her apartment and then saying, *No, stop, I'm sorry, you have to stop.*

In September, Ophélie and Ash moved in together, into Ophélie's apartment. In October, they went shopping for engagement rings and wedding bands. Sitting across from the sixtysomething salesperson at Spence, they held hands, Ophélie's right in Ash's left, the sizing tool with its two dozen clinking aluminum rings hanging off the fourth finger of her left hand.

"You should just get me this one," she said, laughing. "It's shiny and silver. I like it."

The woman across from them smiled. Ophélie slid the ring sizer off her finger.

"Six point five," Ophélie said.

"Great. We have so many options for you, from traditional to more modern. Have you thought about stone shape and size?"

"Not really," Ophélie said.

"I want her to get whatever she wants," Ash said.

"Good man," the sales clerk replied. "He's a keeper," she said to Ophélie.

After trying on pear-shaped diamonds, round sapphires, and matching wedding bands, Ash excused himself to go to the washroom. The salesperson asked when the wedding was, how they'd met.

"I hit Ash with my car."

"What?"

Ophélie laughed. "It's the best story. I'm a nurse, so I drove him to the hospital after. There was a long wait in the ER, so we had time to fall in love."

"That's beautiful," the salesperson replied. "Here, try this one."

The diamond solitaire she held out was of a significantly larger diameter than anything else they'd looked at.

"Oh, that's too much," Ophélie said as she slipped it onto her finger.

"Oh, honey, but you deserve a carat. You know that, right?"

Ash returned then, and Ophélie slid the heavy ring off her finger, telling the sales clerk they'd be back in the next week or two, after they'd had time to think. But she never did go back, even when Ash suggested it.

They didn't discuss their engagement for a few weeks after that, until, one cold November day, flipping through the wall calendar in the kitchen, Ash pointed to a week at the beginning of December.

"I think I should go to India here," he said. "I can get you a ring in Hyderabad."

"You need to go all the way to India to get it? You can't just go to Park Ex?" Ophélie asked, looking up at him from the kitchen table, her fork paused over her plate of scrambled eggs. Ash was standing close to the window, his frame darkened against the bright day's light, the sun's reflection off a fresh layer of snow.

"I don't need to. I want to," Ash said. "It'll be nice to go back to where my family is from and get it there. And there's another piece of jewellery I'd like to buy you—a traditional wedding-day gift from the groom to the bride."

After an hour on the phone with his parents, the trip details were finalized. Ash's mother would already be in Hyderabad, visiting her siblings. Ash would land on a Tuesday, go with her to buy the ring and the mystery item on the Thursday, then spend a solo weekend in Mumbai before returning home.

"And I'm not allowed to just google 'traditional jewellery Indian wedding'?" Ophélie asked.

"No. Absolutely not," Ash said with a laugh.

Ash texted Ophélie from Frankfurt, then Delhi, and then called the night he got in to Hyderabad.

"Sorry for having to whisper," he said. "My aunt is asleep on the couch in the next room. I obviously offered to sleep there myself but she wouldn't hear of it."

"You sound tired," Ophélie whispered in response.

"A little," Ash said. From his intonation, Ophélie could picture the exact expression on his face, his broad, brief smile.

"How was the flight?"

"Much better than I remembered. The individual screens help. And the food was much better. I think the last time I flew to India people were still allowed to smoke on planes."

"That can't be true," Ophélie said, and laughed.

"I guess not," Ash replied, laughing as well.

From Mumbai, Ash wrote: *I think I might go to a gay bar here if you're okay with it.* Ophélie, on shift and about to assist a pediatrics resident with a central line, quickly replied with a thumbs-up emoji before putting her phone face down at the patient's bedside. A few hours later, on her break, she saw that Ash had texted multiple times.

2:11 p.m. So I went.

2:12 p.m. I'm glad I did. I'd wanted to support the scene here.

2:15 p.m. Varun, my cousin, the one who's at university here, came too. So I guess I'm out to him now. He seemed pretty cool with it.

2:20 p.m. Élie, I want to bring you here. And our kids, when we have them. This time, I felt like I could fit in here if I tried, if I got to know the place. It feels exciting—not oppressive the way it used to.

2:25 p.m. Before we left Hyderabad my mom took me to her aunt's house, where my grandmother grew up. It had a small anteroom with dozens of family photos on the walls.

2:30 p.m. You know how we're always saying that I don't look like anyone in my family? It turns out I do. I look exactly like my great-grandfather. Like, exactly. All of my old aunts kept grabbing my cheeks and saying so. I saw his photo and it's uncanny.

2:42 p.m. The gay bar was cool. They're really trying.

Ash flew home a few days later, arriving back at their apartment at the same moment as Ophélie, who'd just finished an overnight shift. Ash had slept well on the plane and was elated as he unpacked in front of her, sitting beside her on the floor, next to his suitcase, pulling out first the lac bangles she'd requested, then two fist-sized velvet pouches with the name, address, and phone number of a Hyderabadi jeweller on one side.

Ash cupped the two drawstring purses in his hands.

"The ring is that bright, Indian, twenty-four-karat gold," he said. "With a diamond. For the other thing—I got pearls instead of gold, to the chagrin of everyone. In India, the measure of a man's love for his wife is in how much gold he buys."

"I'm glad. I like pearls better anyway."

Ash reached out to caress her knuckles and then slipped his fingers under her palm. Ophélie squeezed his loose fist. With his other hand, Ash fiddled with the beads of the black pearl mangalsutra through the velvet pouch. He'd bought a leaf pendant for the necklace, as well, that was to be custom-made and delivered later.

"I'm glad we didn't go back to Spence," Ophélie said. "They totally tried to upsell us. I hated it."

Three weeks after Ash's return from India, just before he headed off to a New Year's Eve weekend in Tremblant, Ophélie and Ash had a stupid fight. Ash had left the kitchen cupboards open, which Ophélie hated. He had failed to reseal the bag of coffee beans, which she hated. And then he'd added a tablespoon of vanilla to the whipped cream instead of a teaspoon, and that was the last straw.

"How could you think you'd need that much vanilla?"

"Hey, I'm sorry," Ash said, taken aback.

Ophélie poured out the whipped cream, slamming the cupboard above the sink shut as the soft peaks gathered in the drain.

"It's ruined now. Dessert is ruined now," she said.

They sat across from one another, eating the raspberry cheesecake Ophélie had made. They chewed in silence. The cake was creamy, flavourful, delicious even without the whipped cream, but Ophélie said nothing. The single candle between them flickered.

When Ophélie had almost finished she stood, leaving Ash at the table, mid-mouthful. She scraped the last forkfuls of cheesecake off her plate and ate them as she walked back to the kitchen, then placed her used dish in the sink atop the sea of heavy cream.

The next day, a single suitcase in tow, she paused at the entranceway of their apartment to text him, knowing he was already halfway to the resort. *I'm sorry*, she wrote. *It's no problem. I love you*, he'd texted back.

As Ophélie walked away down Saint-Jacques, she could feel the dark, elongating shadow of her mistake stretch out behind her. But she was seduced forward by a voice that said: *You deserve someone who doesn't leave you alone when you need them, or run away after a fight, someone who doesn't leave jar lids half-screwed on so that the contents fall out onto you after you've told them repeatedly not to, for fuck's sake. You deserve a carat.*

"Trouble in paradise?" Anca asked when Ophélie arrived at her door.

Ophélie didn't answer. Anca motioned for her to come in, and Ophélie stepped past her into the entrance hall. Anca lived in a six-bedroom house in Brossard with her dentist husband; it had taken Ophélie over an hour, using a combination of the orange line and two buses, to get there.

"You're sure it's okay if I stay here for a few days?"

"Oh, yikes," Anca said, leading her into the kitchen. "I mean, of course. But things are that bad?"

"They're not good," Ophélie replied. She heard her voice echo through the house; she had the surreal sense that she was play-acting the injured spouse, that none of this was real and therefore no harm could come of it.

Anca poured a cup of tea for Ophélie, then one for herself.

"What happened?"

Ophélie took a sip. "Nothing really 'happened,'" she said.

What she didn't say: *Our relationship was getting colder and colder, by half a degree, by a tenth of a degree, until, seemingly suddenly, it froze.*

Only years later—after telling everyone she'd moved on, after so much time had elapsed that when the question was asked the intended object was no longer even Ash, but Lucas, after counselling, and a round of anxiolytics, and treatment for what turned out to be PTSD—did Ophélie begin to understand the weekend she'd left Ash and what had brought her to it, the second-biggest mistake of her life.

There was the day she and Ash had waited in line at IKEA, the three times she'd told him, *It's aisle twenty-eight and bin sixty, okay?* And then the fact that she'd completely lost it on him, her heartbeat loud in her ears, when he'd gone the wrong way.

There was her scared *Oh my God* whenever he dropped something and it made a loud noise.

She'd screamed at him, one night, for having overly dimmed the lights as they'd sat down on the couch to read.

Ophélie tried to fix it. She wrote in her journal every morning, *Be gentle and kind*. But she couldn't.

What Ophélie realized: that the reasons she'd cited to herself on the day of her departure weren't the real reasons at all. That she'd been certain—for weeks, months beforehand—that her erratic behaviour was eroding Ash's love for her. That she couldn't bear to be without him, but that more unbearable would be to slowly bludgeon their relationship to death, to have him think less of her, a little less each day, until nothing remained of his affection. To have him one day remember her as less than the capable, generous woman he had met.

So she left. And even later, when she was better—when she'd talked through almost killing a patient with a therapist, when the anti-anxiety medication was finally able to still her—still, the memories of how she'd wronged him burned as if she'd swallowed them whole, and she didn't call.

Even though she knew Ash would forgive her everything, even her leaving of him, if she asked.

Ophélie met Lucas on Bumble five months after her breakup with Ash, in the late spring of 2018. Lucas had left his wife and infant son in 2010 when he was deployed to Afghanistan, and when he'd returned in 2011 it was to complex regional pain in his right foot—his fourth and fifth toes had been blown off by an improvised explosive device—divorce papers, and an eighteen-month-old who didn't know who he was.

Ophélie and Lucas stayed in, watching *The Handmaid's Tale* and *The Americans*. They ordered poutine from La Banquise, which was across the street from Lucas's place, after having spent the afternoon in his bed. Ophélie would use the ten minutes he was out getting their food to look around his spare apartment, at the few books on the tan particleboard shelves, the master suite that had been converted into a space-themed bedroom for his now eight-year-old son.

Four months in, Lucas invited her to his son's ninth birthday party, a joint princesses-and-robots affair with a neighbour's daughter that was to take place at his ex-wife's. Ophélie made it as far as the front door of the bungalow on Cunard, close enough to hear the squeal of a toy laser gun and the shrieks of a group of girls, before texting Lucas: *It feels like too big a deal, to meet him. To meet her. I don't think I can do this.*

They stayed friends. Lucas sent her a pair of crystal crescent-moon earrings for Christmas; Ophélie sent him and his son chocolate Easter eggs from her favourite chocolaterie on Duluth. He was the first person she told when she was diagnosed with PTSD in June.

When Ophélie texted him the news, Lucas called immediately.

"It totally makes sense," he said, not even saying hello. "I've never met another woman who was happy to just sit on the couch and watch TV with me."

They laughed.

"Are you in treatment?" he asked.

"I am—I took a six-month leave from work and am seeing a psychologist. We're doing exposure therapy."

"That helps a lot."

"First I look at the word *epinephrine*," Ophélie joked. "Then I'll get to draw it up. One day I'll be able to inject someone with it again."

Lucas laughed. "That does seem like a pretty key skill for a nurse."

They started spending two or three hours every night on the phone. Lucas told her about Kandahar: how a thin film of red-gold dust, the sand of the desert, came to cover everything, from his shoes to his desk; how the loud, mechanistic whip of helicopter blades would compete with the peaceful pulse of his ceiling fan as he lay in bed in the early morning; of the R and R, two weeks every six months, the transit through Dubai on his way back to Canada, the glassy infinity pools and on-demand champagne that made him feel even lonelier than lying alone in his bunk did. Of how he'd been looking at a photo the other day, of a half-dozen or so men from his company, and hadn't been able to remember which man had died in the roadside bomb—a stack of anti-tank mines had vaporized his vehicle in an explosion heard for miles—and which had died from small-arms fire when they'd attempted to clear a nameless village in Panjwai.

"You have real PTSD," Ophélie said one night.

"You have real PTSD, too," Lucas replied. "Didn't you just say you had to sit alone in the bathroom for ten minutes any time you saw a patient who had any kind of allergy?"

Her first overnight shift back from leave was on New Year's Day, in the ER at the Montreal Children's Hospital. It was her third move in as many years—she'd transferred from the adult ER at the Royal Victoria Hospital to the ward at the Children's when she'd realized she preferred pediatrics, and then to the pediatric ER when she'd realized she missed the ER.

That night, she was sitting at the nursing station when Lucas walked over to her with his son, Stéphane, who was in his arms and looked unwell. Lucas, to whom she hadn't spoken in three months.

Not recognizing her, Lucas said, "They said to take him to room four, but I'm not sure where that is."

"Hey, it's me," she said. "Ophélie."

"Wow, of course, hi," he said, smiling now, reaching out to touch her elbow as best he could while still holding Stéphane. "You look the same. I didn't realize you were back at work. Honestly, I'm so worried right now I wouldn't recognize my own face."

Ophélie walked them the short distance to room four. She'd gleaned from social media that Lucas was spending more time with his son: on the weekends, as before—father-son days he'd always guarded, even at the expense of seeing her—but also, now, on weekdays. He'd posted photos of macaroni-and-cheese dinners on Tuesdays, of the trunk of his car frozen shut and Stéphane's hockey gear stuck inside one early Thursday morning. His ex-wife had commented on this photo, as on others, with varying gradations of smiley-face emojis, so Ophélie deduced that his relationship with her, cordial but never warm, had improved, too.

"The doctor will be here soon, but what's wrong? The triage note says abdominal pain, and I see he has a fever."

"Yes. And vomiting. And he hasn't eaten anything for days."

Lucas laid Stéphane on the bed and covered him with a blanket.

The boy immediately closed his eyes and rolled onto his side to face the wall.

"We'll fix him. And if you need anything, I'm right here." Ophélie placed a hand on Lucas's upper arm. She looked over at Stéphane, curled into a tight ball, his breathing fast, the movement of his chest visible from the doorway.

"Better not give him anything to eat or drink until the resident sees him," she said, sliding the door closed.

Once Stéphane had been diagnosed with appendicitis, Ophélie went to put in an IV. She gave him a dose of morphine and then sat in the corner with Lucas, explaining the next steps. She walked with them up to the OR, texted when she got home to see how things had gone, and visited Stéphane's bedside the next morning prior to his discharge. He'd been asleep, his mother sitting beside him. She'd said, *Ah, you're Ophélie*, and placed her hand on her son's forearm.

Partway through her shift later that afternoon, Lucas tracked her down to say goodbye. He wore a goose-down jacket and an aviator hat, his cheeks and nose red from the January cold.

"We're parked just outside," he said. "But I wanted to say thank you."

"Oh, you're welcome," she said.

Lucas continued. "I know you said no, last time," he said. "Three months ago. But I wanted to ask you again, because as you and I both know, life is short."

The deep blue of his irises were accentuated by his light green neck warmer. Ophélie looked instead at his cheek, with its brown-and-grey stubble, at the bow of his upper lip.

"Go out with me," he said. "Properly. As my girlfriend."

At Ophélie's answer, his lips turned up at the corners briefly. He reached out a gloved hand to touch her shoulder. And then he turned, walked through the acute care zone, and left the ER through an empty treatment room.

She'd said no again. This time, as she'd said it, she'd thought of Ash, of the last communication she'd had from him, which she'd kept on her phone, now at the bottom of her messages, dated two years ago exactly: *Just got home and read the letter you left me. I can fix this. Please let me.*

A text she'd left on her phone not as a reminder of their love, but as a reminder of how much she'd hurt him.

Two years later, after a first date that had gone particularly poorly, and had ended with her pinned between her suitor and a closed door just outside Café Cléopâtre, his tongue pushed into her mouth and gyrating against her teeth, Ophélie tried to find Ash.

She'd taken Anca's phone off of the nursing station counter—Anca had left it there, face down, while she'd gone to the bathroom—opened Facebook, and searched for Ash's name. Besides confirming to her that he was still alive, his public profile hadn't told her much else. Later, at home, she'd looked for him on Instagram, but he had a private account. She avoided LinkedIn, afraid he'd be notified that she'd sought him out. She considered calling his parents, or his brother, but didn't know what to say: *Hey, I'm looking for Ash, though I couldn't tell you why, or what I'd say to him if I found him. Also, sorry for breaking his heart and ruining his life*. Once, on a whim, she'd called him from the hospital over her lunch break, his number still memorized—knowing that it would read on his end as an unknown number and that if she had to, she could hang up—but his number was no longer in service. She'd even gone through the preliminary steps of hiring a private investigator—to see if she could organize an "accidental" crossing of paths—but when she'd received the formal contract by email, had gotten cold feet.

Then, after a concert at Osheaga, in the crush of people making their way back to the Metro station, she saw him, walking next to someone, pushing a stroller. He was so close she could see the ring on the fourth finger of his left hand.

Ophélie ducked into an alcove. Her cheeks felt tight. A hard kernel was stuck in her throat. She kept her eyes on the pavement—as if being unable to see Ash would somehow make it less likely that Ash would see her—until the crowd receded. Then she made her way to Jean-Drapeau station, alone.

When Ophélie finally did properly meet Stéphane, she was thirty-six and he was fourteen. He and Lucas lived in the same apartment as before, now with a VR headset on a shelf next to the TV and vintage skateboards affixed to the walls. She and Stéphane sat awkwardly across from one another on the living room couches while Lucas poured Ophélie a glass of water in the adjoining kitchen.

Stéphane cleared his throat. "So, you're a friend of my dad's from when he got back from Afghanistan?"

"A little bit after that," Ophélie said. "And then we lost touch a few years ago, with the pandemic and everything."

Lucas came back into the room, smiling broadly. He set the glass down on a coaster in front of Ophélie and sat next to his son. Lucas was so tall and the couch so low that his knees jutted above his hips.

"You look like you were on your way somewhere," Lucas said, with a nod toward the backpack she'd set down near the front door.

"It's my work stuff. I had an errand to run out here after my shift," Ophélie said, lying about the errand. "And then I saw you through the window. So I thought I'd ring the bell and say hi."

She didn't say, *I don't know what brought me to your door after all these years.*

"Well, do you have dinner plans? I've made a bolognese. Stef here has made the pasta."

"I'd love to stay," she said.

They ate the tagliatelle on the balcony—newly repaired by Lucas, who in the last four years had gone back to school and used his experience as an army construction technician to become a general contractor—with one bottle of wine and then half of a second. Stéphane, at some point, retired to one of the living room couches, and soon Ophélie could hear video game machine-gun fire and heavy footfalls.

"You're okay to overhear that stuff?"

"Yeah," Lucas said, stacking his plate under hers and inching his chair slightly closer. He extended his leg until it was touching hers and then curled his toes under the arch of her foot. Ophélie brought her arm to rest on the wrought-iron table, her fingertips just brushing his.

"I'm much better now. Not like I was before I went to Afghanistan, but not nearly as much of a wreck as when I got back."

"Are you still in the army?"

"I left the regular force but I'm still in the reserves. It's great. I get to see some of the guys, do training exercises, stay in that world, but still focus on my contracting business. And, of course, Stéphane. I'm settling down."

Below them, on Rachel, crowds were starting to gather across the street for poutine. Ophélie heard the smash of glass against the pavement, a raised voice. It was midnight; the rest of the apartment was silent. Stéphane had gone to bed.

"Stéphane likes you," Lucas said suddenly. "I always knew he would."

He squeezed her hand and stood, carrying the plates back to the kitchen. Ophélie followed with the empty wineglasses.

"It turns out 2019 was a great time to go back to school," he said. "And, even post-pandemic, we've been flooded with work.

Bathroom upgrades, gut renovations, that kind of thing. I imagine you were pretty busy, too?" he joked.

"Ha, yes," Ophélie said.

"What's the worst thing you saw?" he asked, turning on the faucet and soaping a sponge. "If you feel comfortable answering."

"Well, there's about a hundred-way tie for first place in that category," she said. "Especially when we were called over to help on the adult side. Early in the pandemic I saw a young woman restrained by hospital guards. She'd missed the death of her mother by five minutes and wasn't allowed back in the room to see her. She was on the floor, weeping, because she hadn't gotten to say goodbye. It was the look on the guards' faces as they held her back that I remember, even more than hers."

Ophélie took the dishtowel that was hanging over the edge of the sink and started drying a plate.

"I don't know why I picked that story, out of all of them," she said.

After a glass of port each, taken standing across from one another in the kitchen, Lucas walked Ophélie to the front door, where he handed her her backpack. And as Ophélie reached for it, grabbing the other strap, Lucas pulled both it and her toward him, gently, folding his arms over her shoulder blades and across her back, crushing the blue canvas bag between them as he kissed her.

NAOMI

When she'd escaped at eighteen, it wasn't to anywhere far: just over the border to Pullman, on a swimming scholarship to Washington State. Her parents, a cattle rancher and a housewife, would have struggled to afford university, so from tenth grade on—having progressed through the Red Cross levels into lifeguarding and competitive swimming—Naomi spent early morning and late afternoon in Prince George's public pool, working on her butterfly and front crawl.

Pullman was at best a lateral move, but Naomi took satisfaction in the longer drive—almost fourteen hours compared to the nine it took her other university-bound classmates to get where most of them were going, Vancouver—and in needing a passport and a visa. That, and the fact that she didn't know a soul for miles, made her feel as if she'd gone further than she had.

She'd done well enough at college swimming to keep her scholarship. She'd done even better in her classes, so much so that after her undergraduate degree she won a Commonwealth Scholarship and made it even further away, to Oxford—all the way to another country, another continent.

Naomi did so well at swimming—in school, perhaps, too—thanks to Adderall. Her first dose was given to her by her coach, Francis, just before a swim meet. He'd pulled her into the pool's family locker room and pressed an orange pill into her palm. *This is a caffeine pill*, he'd said. *It'll give you a little boost and it isn't banned. It probably should be, but it isn't.* She'd taken it, mostly because he'd been standing there expectantly with a small plastic cup filled with water, but after the competition—after she'd been first off the blocks and had felt her streamlined shape tear through the water like a bullet, her mind pressing her eagerly on—she'd asked for more. He'd given her a baggie of five pills, and when she took them back to her dorm and poured them out on her desk, she saw *Adderall XR 20 mg* printed on the side of each capsule.

After she finished all five—she'd started using them at practices, as well as during exams—she went back to Francis. He said he had none left, but told her to go to the campus health clinic and act distractible and forgetful. *I think everyone at this school is on these*, he said. *Not just the athletes. If anything, we're just evening the playing field.*

Naomi looked up the symptoms of ADHD online before her appointment. Filling out the intake form, she failed to check either the M or F box that sought to determine her sex. Under Address she put her email address, then scratched it out, writing her campus mailbox number underneath. In with the doctor, she asked him twice to repeat a question, as if she hadn't heard it. She paused mid-sentence after a bird landed on the windowsill, pretending she'd forgotten what she was about to say. Her final statement, *I have a hard time paying attention in class*, was almost unnecessary, the physician having already pulled out his pad to prescribe her the stimulants, to be taken once a day for a month, three repeats.

Soon she was using them to study. Soon she was using them twice a day, staying up late to perfect her assignments. She lost weight, which only made her more beautiful. She was asked out by the boy she liked, only to say no, as she wouldn't have had time to go back to her room and take another pill before their date.

Naomi was careful not to swim too well at her meets; the last thing she needed was to break a school record or advance past the conference level and start being subjected to random drug tests she couldn't prepare for. The way it was, Francis mailed her weekly samples—of what she assumed was his own pee—to store in her dorm-room refrigerator and then provide to the university's biweekly anti-doping program.

Francis, frustrated that her times hadn't improved as much as he felt they should have, pushed her by running her through drill after drill, a new parallel exercise regimen doing power lifts at the gym, appointments with the college dietician. Still Naomi refused to best twenty-three seconds for the fifty-yard free and twenty-four seconds for the fifty-yard fly, as if the artificially rapid beat of her heart were a stopwatch she could count by, and not a ticking time bomb.

Her goal wasn't to win; her goal was to remain escaped from Prince George, in fact, to never set foot there again.

Naomi's parents were able to visit her once in the two years she was at Oxford. She'd seen them infrequently even in the years prior: in the fall when they'd come down to Pullman for Thanksgiving, and again in the spring when she'd meet them halfway, in Vancouver, for Easter. In Oxford, Naomi had them stay with her, in her one-bedroom apartment, giving her parents her bed while she slept on the couch, as if the increased intimacy of so many days of close proximity could compensate for the years she hadn't been back home.

"You missed your five-year reunion, honey," her mother said. They were out at a café that she and Naomi's father had discovered the previous day walking around Oxford and had loved for its scones.

Naomi knew this; her best friend from high school, Andrea, had been on the organizing committee and had sent her the Evite. She'd replied *Maybe*, knowing this would invite fewer questions than *No*. Then she'd booked herself a weekend vacation in Paris over the same dates.

"There was a photo in the *Citizen*," her father said.

In Paris, she'd googled her high school classmates to see where they'd ended up: Chelsea lived with her husband and three children in Kelowna and worked as an occupational therapist; Alan, her first crush, had no existence online except for a CBC article titled "Alan Fairchild from Revelstoke, BC, Located in Alberta," with the subtitle "Twenty-four-year-old Missing Since Thursday Night"; Ben was killed in a snowboarding accident, in an avalanche, after going off-trail at Whistler. Ben had told her, during musical theatre rehearsal in the seventh grade, that her legs were gross and that she ought to shave them; Naomi still recalled the moment, the memory drawn sharp by shame, that he'd taken his hand and run it up her shin, the soft, dark hairs standing upright in his wake, the faded transparency for "We're Off to See the Wizard" askew on the overhead projector, the singing voices surrounding them. She'd shaved her legs with her mother's razor that same night, but Ben had never touched—or even looked at—her legs again. His fate had been easy to determine—a quick Facebook search had taken her immediately to his memorial page. She'd looked for him first, even before her friend or her crush.

Naomi performed this exercise hoping, of course, that none of her classmates had made it as far out of Prince George—either symbolically, by pursuing an advanced degree at one of the world's oldest universities, or physically, by moving seven thousand kilometres away from it—as she had.

Naomi had gotten a full reunion recap from Andrea: *Remember Ashleigh, from the other Grade 12 class? The one who left her husband for the Canucks forward and moved to Vancouver for him? Well, that's over. Jess—remember her from the senior play?—showed me all these Instagram photos of the two of them that Ashleigh had deleted. Ashleigh's had so much plastic surgery, oh my God. Jess does dinner theatre in Calgary now. She says hi. Oh, and do you remember our English teacher, Mr. Sunderland? I ran into him last weekend at the farmers' market. He was asking about you.*

At fifteen, three of Naomi's friends had already had sex and described it to her in great detail. Despite this—and movies, and the internet—gaps in her knowledge remained: *How did one go from wanting to be kissed, Robert Doisneau–style, to having sex?* And: *Do I actually want to have sex, with Mr. Sunderland?*

One day over lunch hour he decided for her. He'd left his office door unlocked with the shades drawn, as he usually did. But this time, instead of screening thirty minutes of a classic film for her—they'd already made it through *King Kong* and *The 400 Blows*, with Mr. Sunderland sitting a few feet away from her at his desk, in his swivel chair—he pulled down her pants, and then her panties, thrusting into her with his fingers until she was wet. He grasped her thighs and pushed her down, onto her knees, onto the vinyl tile, and then stood up from his chair, unzipped his pants, and pushed his penis into her mouth.

A few weeks later he'd been fired, and the rumours flew as to why. That he'd had students into his office over lunch hours was no secret; his office was across from the library on a major school thoroughfare. *He sure was sketchy*, Naomi overheard an eleventh-grader say as she passed her in the hall. *Yeah, but totally hot, too*, her interlocutor had replied. *I'd bang him.*

No one approached her to make a statement. Naomi had done too good a job of sneaking in and out, while Mr. Sunderland had played the snake poised to strike so well that nobody realized he'd been caught on the recoil, having already bitten his victim, delivered his poison.

ROMAN

"Dad, what the eff?" Sasha stood in the open doorway of Roman's office, holding a copy of the *Daily*, his clenched knuckles prominent over the fold of the newspaper. Sasha was in his fourth undergraduate year at McGill, and he'd written for and then edited the paper before he'd dropped his communications minor. Roman knew Sasha still picked up a copy every day, knew that morning—after seeing the article for the first time himself, taped to his office door with the word *JERK* written over it in red—that it would be a matter of hours at most before Sasha saw the article and came by. Roman had only stayed in his office, in fact, to wait for him, both hoping he would and would not arrive.

"I know it looks bad," Roman said. "That they were both students."

"Your students," Sasha said.

"My students. But they were also women, who were adults, who chose willingly, whom I was in love with," he said. "One of them was your stepmother," Roman reminded his son.

"For about two minutes," Sasha shot back. "Naomi was more like a sibling anyway. Only five years older than me, remember?"

Sasha kept a tight grip on the paper, and Roman suddenly recalled the soft curl of Sasha's eighteen-month-old palm around his finger, the slow expansion of his toddler chest against Roman's as they sat on the couch at two in the morning, at their old place in Saint-Henri, the street full of noise from traffic, bar patrons lingering on the sidewalk. Roman had done this every night for three months as his son's teeth were coming in, allowing Kate to rest.

"I don't know what to tell you," Roman said, standing and reaching his hand out toward his son.

Sasha dropped the paper to his side and stepped into the office.

"And this 'chose willingly' thing," Sasha said as he sat down. "We need to talk about that."

Roman had last seen Kate at Sasha's high school graduation. She lived in San Francisco now, remarried to an investment banker. Roman had counted the number of times he'd be likely to speak to her again: Sasha's graduation from university, from law school, his engagement party, his wedding, the birth of each new grandchild. Roman hadn't thought to put *being accused of sexual misconduct and possibly losing one's job* on that list, but Kate called a few days after the *Daily* article came out.

"Hello?"

"Hi, it's Kate."

Roman hated his reaction to the sound of her voice, hated that his love for her remained unchanged from the day she'd walked into the bistro for their first official date, a warm September breeze behind her, worldly and jet-lagged and just home from a business trip to Sydney. Unaltered, even though their last therapy session had ended with Roman yelling, *It's always* me *who takes care of* you, *never you me*, and then, to the therapist, *Did you know she once started backing the car out of the garage before I'd fully gotten in it? It's like she doesn't even see me!*

"Hi," he said.

"I just saw the *McGill Daily* thing," she said. "My mom sent it to me. Now I get why Sasha hasn't returned my calls. He didn't want to tell me, or lie by omission by not telling me."

After their divorce and after years of shared custody—driving Sasha from Saint-Henri to Westmount and back every week, fifty-two times a year—Kate had told Roman, *Oscar wants me to move with him to California. Sasha should stay with you; we both know he loves you more*. Roman had thought, *We both know who loves him more, too*, but stopped short of saying it, a pit yawning open in his chest at the thought of what this, if said out loud, if thought to completion, meant for his son, for the sum total of love he would have in his life.

"Do you need a lawyer, et cetera?" Kate asked. "I still know people. Oscar knows people."

"It'll just be a hearing within the university, I think," Roman said. "No lawyers necessary."

Roman met Kate at a McGill alumni luncheon—he was three years into his PhD, not an alumnus yet, but had tagged along with a friend who was—and ended up in her bed that same afternoon. Sasha was born nine months later.

Roman tried to pinpoint the exact moment he'd fallen for Kate. Was it when he'd first caught sight of her, ahead of him in line at the bar, a half-empty glass of white wine in her hand, her elbow pressed against her hip, the sharp lines of her underwear visible through her grey dress? Was it later that afternoon, in bed beside her, scanning the fifteenth-floor loft for clues, hungry to know her, his gaze falling on the collection of second-hand GMAT prep books stacked under the entrance table—a pile that betrayed how hard she'd fought to get where she was, the more hardscrabble underside to her perfect exterior?

It was in this apartment, with its floor-to-ceiling windows, amidst the wall hangings and statuettes from Japan, after their fifth or sixth date, that Kate had told him she was pregnant. When Roman shared the news with his best friend from high school, his friend had said, *Who isn't on the pill?* To which Roman had retorted, *Who doesn't have a condom in his wallet?*

And Roman knew, he and his friend both knew, with his defence of her, that Roman was all in—and that when Roman and Kate met later that week to discuss next steps, Roman was going to ask Kate to keep the baby.

It wasn't that Kate hadn't wanted to keep Sasha. But she was twenty-four, a month into her third year consulting for McKinsey, and had just applied to do an MBA. And while she knew she liked Roman, she didn't know if they were, in her words, *a forever thing*. In the end, factoring in both Roman's strong preference for as well as her certain misgivings, she cast the deciding vote.

To be honest, I don't think I could have an abortion, she said. *Again.*

Shortly after their first prenatal scan—Roman had held Kate's hand as she lay back in the sonographer's chair, and as the probe passed over the tiny, unexpected embryo, the bounding trampoline of its little heart, Roman squeezed her palm so tightly she withdrew it—they moved in together, into another apartment in Kate's building, a slightly larger loft two floors up that had a corner they planned to turn into a nursery.

"We could set up a four-sided screen here," Kate said, making a zigzag motion with her hand. "That way the baby can have her own space without us having to sacrifice a room. I know a great shop that sells Japanese decor."

"Wait, so none of this stuff is actually from Japan?"

"Well, it still counts as being from Japan even if it's from a store," Kate said.

They married a month after finding out that Kate was pregnant, which was a month before Kate's parents were to visit Montreal. The plan was to announce their elopement, and then the baby, and present the due date as the first of July instead of the first of June.

"She'll be born a few weeks 'early' but that happens all the time," Kate reasoned. "I'm pretty sure my mom was conceived out of wedlock, too, anyway, so I don't think there'll be too many questions. We did a human reproduction unit in biology in high school and I asked my mom if she was born on time, and she stuttered out an 'I think so.' I think so? 'I think so' means Grandma had a really good prom."

At dinner, Kate made a big show of covering her stemmed wineglass with the palm of her hand when the waiter came to the table with the bottle of Barolo. Her mother was the only one who saw her do this; she squeezed Kate's hand, and Kate tapped the edge of her fork against her empty glass.

"So, Mom's noticed already," Kate said.

"Noticed what?" her father replied. "The ring?"

"Not the ring," Kate said.

"What other bad news is there? I've already had to hear that my daughter got married without me," he said.

The three of them laughed, though it wasn't clear if Kate's father was joking.

"I'm not having any wine, even though I love wine," Kate said.

"Oh my gosh," Kate's father replied. "Really? Already?"

Kate nodded. She pulled the sonogram photo out of her purse and handed it across the table to her father, who then leaned over his armrest so his wife could see it.

"Isn't that something," he said, alternating between beaming at them both and staring at the blurry black and white pixels in his hand.

"The obstetrician said it was too early to tell for sure, but that she thinks it's a girl," Kate said.

Roman looked over at her, surprised. He'd been at that appointment; he'd been at every appointment. Nobody had said anything of the kind.

They'd had a pleasant dinner, Kate's father becoming red-faced with Scotch and slinging his arm around Roman's shoulder for the last quarter of the meal. "It won't do any harm if it's not true," Kate said as they were getting ready for bed. "I just knew it would make them even happier to really be able to picture her."

It was only after this initial whirlwind of events that Roman realized everything he'd initially loved about Kate had been, in some way, a pretense. Her worldliness: she'd been to Australia, once, and to Singapore, in transit on the way to Australia. Her beauty: rigorously maintained with makeup classes, a skin-care regimen that took an hour before bedtime, the loathsome daily stepping onto the scale that he heard every morning through the bathroom door. Her ease with others: paid for after every social encounter with hours of *Did they like me? Was I annoying? I think they only invite me because of you.*

But she had qualities he admired, as well, ones he'd discovered contemporaneously and that had dampened his disillusionment. Her ambition to improve herself: how she strove to be the person she projected herself to be. Her love of all living creatures: every dog passed on the street had to be acknowledged, cooed over, petted, every spider cocooned gently in a paper towel and deposited on the balcony. Her spontaneous generosity: the gold pendant she'd gifted to their cleaning lady, just because she'd admired it, one day, on Kate.

In the days after the accusations surfaced, Roman spent hours in his office, hiding, distracted, unable to focus on his work. He stared at his computer screen, his gaze shifting to his bookshelf, then to the dented bronze doorknob, then to the tufted leather chair across from his desk. He counted its every button and crease, noted every irregularity and imperfection. He thought of its provenance: gifted by his father-in-law almost two decades ago as his own career was winding down, for Roman to use in his new job as assistant professor at McGill. Naomi had sat there. The dean of his department had sat there and offered him tenure. Estela had sat there and asked him to tie her wrists with a scarf and hook the knot under one of its feet.

Where had he gone wrong? With Estela, Roman was sure he hadn't: she'd been twenty to his thirty-two, his TAs had marked the student papers, he'd been in love with her. He probably shouldn't have written her a reference letter, but she'd been one of his best students and had deserved one.

What about Naomi? She'd been twenty-four to his forty-six, a student in one of his graduate seminars. She'd wanted a baby, ideally two; he'd said he wasn't ready. He should have said, *The question makes me uncomfortable, and if I were to parse out why, I would realize it has nothing to do with not being ready. The truth is I don't love you enough—that, after Kate, I haven't loved any woman enough—to give you a child when I don't want another one.*

Instead, Roman married her.

So perhaps he did deserve to be accused by Naomi, even if it wasn't for the reason she'd described.

Roman had received angry emails in the past—one from an undergraduate contesting a grade that stated, petulantly, *If I'm a C student it's because you're a C teacher*, one from a graduate student who was so infuriated he'd docked her marks for a late paper that she'd signed off with, *Would you have done this if I were white?*—but these were nothing like the letters that flooded his inbox the day after the *Daily* article appeared.

From a student he'd had a decade or so back, a particularly bright one, one whose name he still remembered and who'd had the courage to send her message from her personal email address: *I had thought better of you.*

From a Gmail account with random numbers and letters as its username: *I hope they strip you of your tenure the way you stripped those women who came to your office hours.*

From an unknown account on Instagram: *Fuck you.*

It was incomprehensible to Roman, still, that of all the girlfriends he'd had since Kate, it was Naomi he'd chosen to marry. His first relationship after the divorce had been Estela, but Roman had decided early to give of himself only partly. He knew he'd disrupt her life, causing her to tack right when her true course lay straight ahead: grad school, a career abroad, a chance meeting on a London park bench that blossomed into love, a beachside wedding, two sons. So Roman had loved Estela, not fully, but on purpose, and too much to tether her to him, a man nearly a decade older who was settled in his tenure, his mortgage, and the son he already had.

So he'd refused to commit, even from the outset—his love an outstretched palm with one finger curled back.

Roman remembered the day—the minute—he pulled away from Estela. It was a warm August evening, late in the one summer they'd had together, and they'd been in his study, the manuscript of his first book laid out on the desk. Roman had left it there intentionally for Estela to find, to impress her.

It had, ironically, been one of the best evenings of his life, in what he now looked back on as one of the best summers of his life. Every word that came to his pen was golden, effortless. He wrote the entire first draft of his second book in three months. He'd made peace with Kate—who, the previous July, had sent their son to a sleep-away camp in Muskoka even though Roman had begged her not to, even though he'd said Sasha could spend the summer with him, that he'd take the time off work for it—and now saw his son every afternoon. And then, of course, there was his affair with Estela, the giddiness of being on the brink of love, the balmy walks they'd taken up Saint-Laurent at night, her hand in his, music blaring through the open car windows of evening revellers.

Estela had stood over the manuscript, frowning, and said, *You count one cosmogony, but I see three more. The Fall, the Flood, and the Second Coming are also creation stories, no?* He'd laughed, kissed the back of her neck, and, a few days later, made the changes she'd suggested directly on the near-final manuscript in black ink, all while thinking, *She's too smart for me, I'll just hold her back, I should break up with her.*

But he didn't. Instead, Roman started seeing Estela three times a week instead of four, then two instead of three, departing after sex instead of spending the night, waiting an hour or two to text her back, and then, by the time October arrived, not texting her at all. Until Estela, hurt and angry, turned up at his doorstep when she knew Sasha would be there—*It's the only time I knew you'd definitely be home*, she'd said—and broke things off herself.

After Estela, Roman dated five women in succession: a criminal lawyer he'd met while on jury duty; a bright, ponytailed early childhood educator who worked at his son's after-school program; a bartender; a friend's cousin; and a performing arts student with a major in circus who looked like a younger, bustier Kate. Then, Naomi.

Roman started dating Naomi in the fall of 2016, not remembering that he had, in fact, already met her that spring. He'd been with the circus artist when Naomi had visited in April to interview for the PhD program. Roman had remembered her photo from her file, said a few kind words about her presentation, ranked her second as a candidate for the PhD, and then forgotten her.

Later that summer, after the trapezist left him—by text, to be the mistress of a Cirque du Soleil manager—Roman saw Naomi's name on the list of accepted candidates, along with the description *Renaissance literature, early modern England, visual arts*. Then her name appeared again, on a list of TAs who'd been assigned to his first-year survey course.

Naomi also registered for his graduate Shakespeare seminar and strode into it, the first day, wearing a navy blue wraparound dress that cinched at the waist and flared down to her knees. Head-on, she was beautiful—nothing like her grainy application photo—and, with her thick eyebrows and bright eyes, lovelier even than Kate.

After a few weeks—watching Naomi take notes in her elegant hand, listening to her draw parallels to Plato, to miscegenation in Faulkner, one afternoon pushing her notepad slightly closer to the student beside her, who'd arrived late, forgotten her book, forgotten her notes—Roman realized that Naomi was an intellectual, like him, and that she gave freely to others, even to near strangers, what Kate would have clutched to her chest.

That she would be a better match for him, a better partner, than Kate ever was.

Roman's first gift to Naomi—for her birthday, in January, four months after they'd started dating—was a fully paid, twelve-month membership to a downtown gym with a twenty-metre pool.

"So you can swim whenever you want," he said. "I bragged to the sales manager that you were a swimming champion in college."

"This was so nice of you. So thoughtful," Naomi replied. "But I don't swim anymore. I needed to to get here, but I never really liked it."

Then she pocketed the membership card, offering no further explanation.

When they moved in together upon their engagement, Naomi threw herself into household duties. She set up a regular schedule of comforts, including sourdough bread, fresh-baked for the week on Sunday mornings, and Thursday-night movie nights, the two of them curled up under a woollen blanket on the couch. She repainted in a warm colour palette: ochre, pollen yellow, hunter green. She adorned their Mile End home with Inuit art on exposed bookshelves, and Turkish rugs, the only oddity in the decor a bright-yellow rubber duck, clearly meant for toddlers but placed by her on the edge of their white porcelain claw-footed bathtub.

She asked him how he felt about everything but communicated indirectly herself: design magazines proliferated on every surface for weeks before she brought up the idea of a kitchen renovation; the rubber duck disappeared after they'd had their first fight, about whether or not to have a child—Roman had said *Another child*, to which Naomi had said, *You have one, I don't have one*—and did not reappear. She refused to talk about ex-boyfriends, ex-crushes, her first kiss, her first sexual experience. When Roman mentioned any former lover, she sat stony-faced and refused to meet his eyes until he stopped.

Roman knew Naomi had ADHD, knew about the pills she'd taken every morning for years, up until their marriage. Sometimes, early in their relationship, when she had a lot of coursework and he'd go to bed before her—her alert eyes flicking up from her screen when he said goodnight past midnight—he'd find her still at her desk at four in the morning when he got up to pee, and then lying on the couch at eight, watching movies in a daze, unable to sleep. And he would wonder if, maybe, she took too many.

The first time she'd ever cried in front of him—in fact, the most emotional he'd ever seen her—was on their wedding night, when she'd told him that the pills made her feel crazy, that she didn't need them anymore, that she was going to stop.

On an earlier evening, in the four months between their engagement and their marriage, Naomi suggested they each make the other a traditional family recipe. Roman went first and made borscht, following his grandmother's notes. Naomi, whose family, many generations back, was from Scotland, made steak and kidney pie. For dessert she made trifle, baking the sponge cake from scratch and adding Jell-O.

"Jell-O?" Roman joked.

"We had to make some concessions to the New World," Naomi said.

The Jell-O they made together. Naomi boiled two cups of water; Roman took the other measuring cup, the larger one, and filled it to the brim with cold water from the sink faucet. They poured the water over the gelatin from opposite sides of the baking dish, laughing, Naomi's engagement ring twinkling in the late-afternoon sunlight, the bracelets around her wrists gently percussive as she added pear and peach cubes from a can into the mixture. She covered the glass dish with plastic wrap and placed it in the fridge; Roman pushed her back against the fridge door the moment she closed it, kissing the line of her jaw, his hand caressing her leg up to, and then under, her dress.

It was Roman's happiest afternoon with Naomi, though the Jell-O, much like their marriage—despite having the perfect ingredients and following the instructions to the letter—never really properly set.

Their courtship had been brief; Roman's affair with Estela had made him bolder. He'd asked his seminar students to submit outlines of their proposed final papers early in the term, the first time he'd ever made such a request in this course. When Naomi responded, he'd replied to her, and only her, asking if she could meet him during office hours to go over her arguments. When she'd replied yes, he'd texted her, suggesting that they meet to discuss over a glass of wine at a tapas bar near campus.

They'd ended up back at his office, both tipsy, close to nine in the evening. The sun had long set, the blinds were fully open, and Roman worried, briefly, that the light from his desk lamp would make them visible from the street.

Then he forgot this. He sat against his desk, facing the closed door, his torso naked. His pants were unzipped but still fastened around his waist. Naomi was in his lap, also facing the door, her violet-print skirt bunched between his abdomen and her back. Roman had his left arm around her chest and was clutching her right breast, pulling her down onto him, his other arm outstretched and pressed against a teetering stack of books, preventing their fall. The desk legs scraped against the vinyl tile, losing an inch of ground with every thrust.

When her intake of breath grew sharper, a groan starting in the base of her throat, Roman turned her over, roughly, his left arm now pinned between her breasts and his desk, jamming the soft pad of flesh at the base of his right thumb into her mouth, the bones of his lower hand gripped between her teeth, dulling her moan. He came, too, seconds later, his cry echoing down the empty hall. The top few books in the pile fell off the corner of his desk, landing with thuds on the floor.

When the transcript of their text messages from that night were read back to him during the university's sexual harassment investigation—including the damning *Let's meet for a glass of wine instead*—Roman denied anything untoward in his intent, forgetting his targeted seduction.

At the beginning of the winter semester, their first together, Naomi just narrowly missed being Sasha's TA. When she saw his last name on the course list she'd been frantic, drafting an email to the English department feigning illness, a benign cyst that needed to be removed and that would require a month-long recovery; she'd put out feelers to the other TAs to see who would be amenable to a potential switch. She couldn't cite a conflict of interest as she and Roman had yet to disclose their relationship. When she asked Roman—before Sasha pulled out of the course at the last minute, saving her—if he'd consider a more formal declaration, he'd said, *We've only been together three months. I love you and I want this, but let's try to find another way?*

Roman finally introduced Naomi to Sasha just before they got engaged, in May. Sasha, who'd been an easygoing child, had grown into an easygoing adult. *Sure, Dad*, he'd said, when Roman asked if he'd like to meet Naomi. *Mom's been remarried for ages; I'm glad you found someone.* Roman didn't mention Naomi's age or the fact that it was possible they'd crossed paths on campus already.

That Sunday, Naomi set the table for brunch outside on the balcony, which had a view out over the Lachine Canal. Sasha arrived with croissants. The two hit it off immediately; Naomi had agonized all morning about what to wear, but now her shoes were kicked off to one side, her legs crossed, her fingers resting on the stem of her wineglass, and they were laughing. Sasha's expression was impenetrable—he was wearing sunglasses—but Roman could tell from the way he sat, from the way he held his limbs, that he was enjoying himself, too.

Roman thought briefly, *I wonder if those two would have gotten together had I not been around.*

He brought out coffee.

"Rome," Naomi said. "I had no idea that Sasha was on the editorial board at the *Daily*."

"And he was their star reporter before that. Here, let me show you," Roman said, setting down her coffee, already mixed with milk, in front of her.

"Dad," Sasha protested.

"Hold on." Roman handed Sasha a cup of black coffee and went back into the living room, returning a few minutes later with a large hardcover scrapbook. He placed it open in front of Naomi. On the left page was a film review; on the right, a story about a petition to the Post-Graduate Students' Society. Naomi turned the page to the next article, "Management Student Expelled for Drug Possession," a two-pager.

"Whoa," she said.

"Yeah, that was actually my first story," Sasha said.

"'Alvin Huang, a first-year international student from China, was expelled earlier this week when an anonymous tip to campus police revealed thousands of dollars in cash and upward of fifty grams of cocaine in his residence desk drawer,'" she read. "Wow."

"Yeah. Students aren't often expelled for drug possession at McGill, but when it became clear he was dealing coke, they threw him out. I don't think he went to jail, but I do think he was sent back to China."

"That's crazy," Naomi said.

Roman sat in the empty chair between them, watching a lone jogger dragging a leashed dachshund on the path by the canal. The sky had turned grey; the air held a light mist.

"I so badly wanted to make the joke about how he'd arrived on campus already possessing the requisite business skills for the degree, but the editor wouldn't let me," Sasha said.

They all laughed. A spear of sunlight broke through the clouds, illuminating Sasha's arm, Naomi's face. And Roman, the sun on his bare knees and an unrelated warmth spreading through his chest, almost ran back into the loft to grab Naomi's engagement ring and propose to her right then and there.

For as long as Roman could remember, he'd had nightmares wherein he lost Sasha. More specifically: in his nightmares, Sasha died, usually through some fault of Roman's. In one, an infant Sasha slipped through the straps of a poorly fastened life jacket on a canoe-camping trip and plummeted to the bottom of the lake. In another, Roman wandered around and around a bazaar, searching for Sasha, only to realize he'd sold him to the highest bidder, only remembering the horrific act of that earlier dream version of himself when he returned to his hotel room and saw the pile of bills on the footstool, the scattered coins on the floor.

The fear that Sasha could die at any moment haunted Roman's waking life as well. As the barista at Starbucks wrote his name in marker on his coffee, Roman imagined a concrete slab crumbling off a roof and crushing one side of Sasha's face. As Roman slipped his left heel into a new left shoe at Simons, he saw, in his mind's eye, his son's undiagnosed brain aneurysm explode.

The death of other children also hit Roman hard. He'd been in his office when he'd seen the photo of the migrants from El Salvador, a father and his daughter. Her little red pants, her waterlogged diaper. The slim blue strap of his boxers just visible above his shorts. The muddy water. Their hair, eerily the same. Roman had cried then, alone at his desk in front of his computer, having worked late in order to be able to tell Naomi that he was working late.

In the middle of the night, that same night, he'd had another nightmare. He was at an athletic complex—Roman recognized it as the YMCA on Stanley but larger, Escher-like in its complexity—with Sasha, who was there for a swimming lesson. There were other parents, laughing children, a clear inflatable floaty shaped like a unicorn around Sasha's waist. Then Roman was in a hallway, talking to another parent but looking for Sasha, vaguely worried he wasn't in sight. Then, in a different hallway, with higher ceilings, fewer parents, and minutes and minutes and minutes, he now knew, since he'd last seen Sasha. Then him running, slamming fire-escape doors that looked like they belonged in a high school, trying to find Sasha, refusing to go near the pool while simultaneously realizing the pool is where he would be.

Roman had awoken, sobbing, to hear Naomi, beside him, sobbing.

"You'd actually stopped breathing," she said, her hand heavy on his chest, her fingertips wiping the tears from the corners of his eyes.

It was three in the morning and he'd still called Sasha, who didn't answer but whose warm recorded voice stating his name, "Alexander Arshovsky," reassured Roman all the same.

Roman and Naomi had been married for six months—together for a year and a half—when Roman realized that Naomi was just a smart, pretty girl, and that he had no more affinity for her than that. She was an intellectual, yes, like him, unlike Kate. He'd witnessed a single act of generosity—when she'd shared her notes with a fellow student—again unlike Kate, and made of this single act the scaffolding upon which he constructed her, his Galatea, his better-than-Kate replacement Kate.

But he didn't love Naomi. He still loved Kate, over twenty years on. And when his lust for Naomi dried up, and, with it, the delusion he'd constructed, and he awoke beside her, day after day, he realized that he did mind the tubes of mascara he was continually knocking over in the bathroom, he begrudged her the loud whir of the blended morning smoothies that often woke him, he hated her constant presence everywhere—always already sitting where he wanted to sit—hated the sound of her voice, ceaseless and plaintive.

They stayed together for a year after that. And then, in February—tired of Naomi's doe eyes in the morning as he leapt out of bed at the sound of his alarm, brushed his teeth in the shower, and took his coffee to go, but, more than anything, simply just tired, from staying out late to avoid her and waking up early to avoid her—he told Naomi they needed to talk.

Roman had prepared his lines. *I'm not a good partner to you, we both know it.* And: *Ever since we married, no, ever since we met, I haven't really been present for you.* Her small attentions, her big hopes, were like weights roped to his ankles.

When Roman and Naomi sat down together, facing each other on opposite couches, she refused to meet his eyes, as if she knew what was coming.

"I think this isn't working for us," he said.

"You mean for you," she said.

After their breakup conversation, Roman went for a walk to give Naomi some space. When he returned to the apartment later that afternoon—he'd hoped, secretly, that Naomi would have found a way to move her things while he was out—he deduced from the single dresser drawer flung open and partly emptied that she'd taken an overnight bag with essentials, just enough for a few days, and gone to stay with a friend.

Roman didn't hear from Naomi again. She hired a moving company to pack the rest of her clothes and the few pieces of furniture that belonged to her, and they arrived, businesslike, at exactly the time they'd auto-texted they were going to arrive, leaving with full boxes ninety minutes later. They even swept the floors, and Roman accepted their business card when it was offered, sticking it to the fridge with a magnet. Sasha was graduating next year, after all, and would need movers at some point.

The apparent ease of their denouement made the email that landed in his inbox a few months later—at the beginning of the fall term—even more shocking.

Dear Professor Arshovsky:

We have received a complaint which makes allegations regarding your conduct. These allegations are serious in nature and pertain to relationships in which you were involved during the 2002–2004 and 2016–2019 academic years. The complaint suggests:

- that you were involved in one or more romantic relationships about which the University was not aware, contrary to university policy;
- that you gave preferential treatment to individuals with whom you were in relationships; and
- that you exchanged academic favours such as grades, academic positions, and reference letters in return for sex and/or sexual acts.

Pursuant to the Policy Against Sexual Violence, McGill University has opened an internal investigation into the above allegations.

You are required to attend an investigation interview on October 11, 2019, at 10:00 a.m. in the James Administration Building, Room 524. The purpose of this interview is to provide you with the opportunity to respond to the allegations that have been made.

Be advised that the above accusations, if deemed true, could result in disciplinary action up to and including termination of your employment. You are required to co-operate fully in this investigation, the details of which you are not permitted to discuss with anyone.

Sincerely,
Maeve O'Neill, Special Investigator
Office for Mediation and Reporting
McGill University

As he did with all official correspondence from the university, Roman printed the letter and placed it in a file folder labelled *Work Admin*. Then—as he would have done for any appointment—he took out his day planner, turned to the relevant week in October, and copied out the meeting details in the small square provided.

Later, flipping back to this page in his planner—even though he'd memorized the details, and he could sense the date approaching as a mollusc senses a needling irritant, forming over it layers of nacre, a small stone to sit in its belly—he saw that his hand had been shaking so much that the reminder he'd written for himself was illegible.

Why had Naomi done it? Their scandalous start had been a joke between them; in bed, even after they were married, she often insisted on playing the hapless student "paying" her TA for an A; certainly there'd never been any indication that she'd felt abused, taken advantage of. Roman knew of an episode in her past, an impropriety in a teacher's office when she was fifteen that she'd only ever alluded to. Was that how she saw him?

Sasha, wearing a dark jacket and a bow tie, was already seated in front of a large seafood tower near the bistro windows when Roman arrived.

This had been Roman and Kate's downtown spot, their go-to for birthdays and anniversaries, when Sasha was young; later, it was the site of the uncomfortable graduation dinner they'd had when Sasha finished high school, with Roman seated awkwardly next to Oscar and across from Kate. Roman had avoided the place since, his stomach as if filled with misshapen rocks whenever he remembered the moment Oscar had snuck away to the bathroom and surreptitiously paid the bill.

"It never ceases to amaze me exactly what you remember from when you were eight years old," Roman said. He sat down across from Sasha with a nod toward the lobster, crab, and shrimp stacked in the middle of the table. "Special occasion?"

"I have big news," Sasha said.

"Ah," Roman said. A waiter poured him a glass of champagne from a bottle stationed in a bucket of ice beside their table. Roman raised his eyebrows.

"I knew you'd be paying," Sasha said. They both laughed. "How's the thing going?"

"Well, I received an official summons," Roman said. "October eleventh. It's terrifying, quite frankly."

Sasha chewed and nodded. "I can't say the narrative down at the student level is great either."

"We'll see," Roman said. He downed his champagne and poured himself another, waving off the waiter who'd started toward their table to refill his glass.

Sasha paused. "Well, as for why we're here," he said. "I've met someone."

For a second his son looked worried: that furrowed brow, that same look he'd had as a child when he'd be caught out in a lie, or as when he'd been left at the classroom door on his first day of kindergarten and said, *Will Daddy come later to get me?*

"It's a guy," Sasha said.

For a moment they were both silent. Sasha was tapping his middle finger, rapidly but almost imperceptibly, against the white tablecloth.

"That's wonderful. Congratulations," Roman said, lifting his champagne flute. "You know I knew you were gay, right?" he said.

Even though he hadn't, not really.

By the end of lunch, the early autumn sun warm on their forearms, both tipsy from the bottle of champagne, Roman had invited Sasha and his boyfriend over for dinner that coming Saturday.

"What's his name?"

"Ashish. Ashish Kaza. He goes by Ash, though."

"That sounds vaguely familiar. Did he go to McGill? You mentioned he's a bit older?"

"He did. He studied poli-sci and history, though, so I'm not sure you would've crossed paths."

"Huh," Roman said, motioning to the waiter for the bill.

Roman determined, a few days later, how and through whom he'd known Ash. He was on his couch, watching *Interview with the Vampire* on cable, when he remembered Estela, seventeen years ago now, telling him it was her favourite book. They'd been sitting on the lawn in front of the Redpath Museum, an exaggerated three feet apart. They hadn't been sleeping together yet, but now, looking back, Roman realized he'd already been in love with her.

Ash had walked up to their spot on the grass, eyeing the space between them, and held a hand out to Roman.

I'm Estela's best friend, Ash, he'd said. Estela had looked surprised, either at the title *best friend* or at Ash's sudden appearance, Roman wasn't sure.

Roman remembered a scrawny Indian kid with large glasses, an over-heavy backpack on his shoulders as if he were going to a summer camp. He remembered that Ash had clearly been in love with Estela.

That same kid—whose hand Roman had shaken bemusedly when it was offered—was now so seriously involved with his son that Roman was to meet him, and that they had each changed course for the other, with Sasha now heading to Concordia for graduate school because Ash had cancelled his next posting, in Albania, for him.

When his condo doorbell rang that Saturday, Roman answered it still wearing his apron. He kissed Sasha on the cheek, then held out a hand to Ash, an oddly symmetrical gesture to the one Ash had made all those years before. Roman studied his eyes for any sign of recognition but found none.

"The meatballs are still in the oven." Roman took Ash's jacket and helped Sasha out of his. "But the wine has been decanted."

"Wonderful. Thanks, Dad," Sasha said. "I'm so happy you two are meeting."

"Me too," he said, leading them into the kitchen.

"My dad makes this incredible meatball dish with ground chicken and sherry," Sasha said, reaching for Ash's hand.

Roman added cream to the stock and stirred.

"So, Alex tells me you're a professor at McGill," Ash started. Roman looked up. Their eyes met. Here it was. "You look familiar. I think we might have met once or twice while I was there."

"That's definitely possible," he said.

Ash lowered his chin in a tiny nod that lasted just a second. Roman nodded back. He exhaled.

"Then again, maybe not," Ash said. He raised one of the glasses of wine Sasha had poured and left on the counter.

"Maybe not," Roman replied. "Oh, and if you want to join the family, you're going to have to start calling him Sasha."

Later, his face animated, Sasha raised his empty glass toward Roman, who was in the kitchen looking for the dessert spoons. Roman lifted a third bottle of wine, not yet opened, into the air in response, but felt a sudden ache for the two-year-old body to which that gesture belonged, of toddler Sasha raising an object of interest straight above his head and holding it there, for the specific shape of Sasha at that age, the bulging cheeks, his bold, unsteady gait.

Roman walked out of the James Administration Building and headed toward the English department's offices. The special investigator had been candid at the end of the hour-long interview, stating that, given the written report he'd already provided and the new information she'd gleaned from their meeting, she would find Roman guilty of sexual harassment—there was no way out of that, with Roman having had sex with his own students in his campus office—but, given that Estela was no longer at McGill and his affair with Naomi had resulted in marriage, both she, and the dean of the Faculty of Arts, who would make the final pronouncement on his punishment, would be lenient.

The interview itself had been brutal. There were two complainant letters, Naomi's and Estela's, and a third supporting document, from an unnamed friend of Estela's, that had been expected but was never mailed in. Naomi's letter was vitriolic to the point that the special investigator, who had read it out loud, was visibly uncomfortable, but the true shock had come in Estela's. Estela had slid in, almost as an aside, that due to the unexpected nature of their first sexual encounter she'd had an abortion the November of her third year, and that she'd "suffered significant emotional distress" in the days and months afterwards.

In the departmental meeting scheduled immediately after Roman's hearing—which had as its ostensible topic a curriculum update, though Roman felt that he was the only subject under scrutiny—he realized that while he might have kept his job, albeit with a reprimand and a requirement to undergo counselling, he'd lost his colleagues' respect. And, in the case of some of the men—those who kept their eyes averted, who fiddled with the lids of their pens sooner than look at him, individuals he knew had maintained their own trysts with students, even while married—that he had fallen in their regard not because of his misconduct but because he'd gotten caught. The head of his department—a woman in her fifties who had always hated him—appeared triumphant.

After the departmental meeting, back outside in the crisp fall air, Roman felt his phone vibrate in his pocket. He knew it was Sasha but waited until the call went to voice mail. Then he pulled out his phone and opened Facebook Messenger.

He started composing a message to Estela. *I just got out of my hearing. I am so sorry for what I put you through. With the abortion. I had no idea*, he wrote. He paused, deleted his words, and started again. *I understand why you felt you had to do this,* he wrote, even though he didn't. *And I hope it's okay that I'm writing to you, but if it isn't, just don't write back. I'll understand*. He hit Send, then continued: *Does it make it any better that I was truly in love with you?*

He looked at her profile, at the photos she'd made public. He saw that she'd gotten married and changed her name to Estela Tiessen. Her profile picture was from a pregnancy photo shoot: a tall man stood behind her, with his hands over hers, on her belly. He looked at a few recent posts as well, including one that showed a cupcake cut in two to reveal a pink centre, with the hashtags #BabyGirl and #BabyPatricia.

He went back to his message to Estela and saw three dots appear, indicating she was replying. Then they disappeared.

A month later, with still no response received, he archived the message.

KATE

Kate saw the number on her cellphone's display screen and rejected the call, snapping the phone shut. It was the third call from the same number that week; she knew who it was but refused to add his name and number to her contacts on principle.

At first it had been her calling him, initially once a week to set up meeting times, then almost daily to inquire as to why he was late, or ask when she'd be getting the photocopies of the previous exams he'd agreed to provide, or to tell him that his printout of algebra questions was illegible, the *x* barely distinguishable from the *y*. Then, after her GMAT score refused to budge above 520 despite doubling the frequency of their tutoring sessions, and Demetri's sister Larissa borrowed Kate's ID and did the third test attempt for her, the balance of power shifted, and suddenly he was calling her.

First it was for money, the ten thousand dollars he'd charged to have Larissa sit the exam for her. Then it was another five hundred dollars for "related costs." Then he started to call her weekly, then multiple times a week—phone calls that, her debt having been discharged, Kate chose not to answer.

Demetri, though eventually extortive, had been a good teacher. He'd gathered interesting texts from *The Economist*, asking her to choose between five summaries, each subtly different, that he'd written out by hand. He composed preposterous math questions that made her laugh: *Ruth, Luke, and Mark go to Burning Man. They spend sixty dollars on condoms for the first two nights. On the third day, they meet Judith, Esther, and Paul and really hit it off. Everyone is bisexual. How much should they spend on condoms for the next two nights?* He shared old exams that Kate devoured.

One of his test-prep tips she still used every day, even decades later: while waiting in line to pay at the drugstore—at any store, really—she'd add up the cost of her purchases in her head, calculate and then add the 15 percent tax, and hand the person at the register exact change.

Kate exulted in the cashier's stunned look, in her mind's agility with the numbers—daily proof that, despite having cheated, she deserved her MBA, her high-powered job, her luxurious life.

That September, a week after she'd received her score—a 720, assuring her the MBA program she'd wanted—Demetri called and this time she'd answered, his surprised, upturned *Hello?* to her firm, cold *Hi*, to which she'd replied, *What, what do you want now, my kidney?* after which they both recalled he had the upper hand and he'd said, laughing, *No, not your kidney. The rest of you, definitely. Have dinner with me?*

In the fall of her final undergraduate year at McGill, Kate had ended up in a hospital bed at the Royal Vic with a ruptured ovarian cyst. She'd been at an outdoor yoga class on Lower Field when she'd collapsed onto all fours, her left hand pressed to her right lower abdomen, the pain sudden and sharp as if a long pin had been inserted into her side. Charlotte, beside her, had called a taxi, and she and another girl from their yoga class had helped Kate into it, her friend climbing in beside her through the rear door on the driver's side.

"Your ovary might have gotten twisted," Charlotte said, on the slow drive up University. "That happened to me last year and that's exactly how it feels."

Later, alone, her bed at an uncomfortable thirty-degree angle, an IV in her left arm and another tube emptying her bladder, Kate saw the nurse come in first every hour, then every half-hour, and then every fifteen minutes to check her vital signs. Then she passed out and woke up in a different room with a different nurse.

"Let me get the resident," the nurse said when she saw that Kate had come to.

Her right side ached, but differently. She had six missed calls from her mother. From the time and date on her phone, she realized she'd been there overnight and it was now the next day.

A woman wearing boxy green scrubs a size too large came into the room and sat on the side of Kate's bed.

"I'm Dr. Alcoba," she said. "We had to take you to the OR. You were bleeding internally from the ruptured cyst. Everything went well. We stopped the bleeding and were able to remove the cyst and save both ovaries."

The resident continued, clearing her throat.

"We noticed something else. Your Fallopian tubes are enlarged and bulbous. They're supposed to be thin and straight," she said.

"We usually only see that after PID. Have you had PID before?"

"What's PID?"

"Oh, sorry," the resident said. "Pelvic inflammatory disease. You can get it after getting an STD, like chlamydia or gonorrhea."

"No," Kate said. "I haven't, not that I know of," and as soon as she said it remembered the urinary tract infection she'd thought she had, and the antibiotic she'd taken for it that had brought no relief, until the pain resolved on its own a couple of weeks later.

"I wanted to mention it as it might affect your fertility, later," the doctor said.

When she'd said to Roman, standing next to him as they'd looked out her loft windows, toward the Ferris wheel at La Ronde lit up in yellow and slowly turning, *I don't think I could have an abortion, again*, what she didn't say was, *What if this is my only chance?*

The list of things Kate had kept hidden, both from herself and from others: her shadowy memories of her first few years—her birth mother's long blond hair, the scent of her shampoo, the faded rose-patterned swaddle cloth in which she herself must have been wrapped, and that she'd bundled her own stuffed animals in; the sound of the train going past the trailer park, her toddler chair vibrating, the rise in her throat as she ran to the window to see it; the blank place in her memory which must have been her mother leaving, the arrival of Children's Aid, and her move to her new home, with her new parents; the afternoon she'd spent learning to vomit, her fingers in the back of her throat further than she'd realized they needed to go, the three hours it had taken her to finally have the courage to do it, and the secret, kept until this day, that, despite the in-patient treatment, the outpatient treatment, the day program, even twenty years later she would have preferred being skinny and miserable to being healthy and happy; the three weeks when she was sixteen, having heard her adoptive mother cry through the door of the upstairs bathroom at another failed pregnancy test, another failed round of IVF, and, fearing a biological child would erode their love for her like locusts would erode ancient fields, she'd taken the birth control pills the school nurse had handed out for free and put them in her mother's morning coffee, one every day for twenty-one days. Her fear that she, not her mother's poor ovarian reserve and the fact that she was forty-two, was the cause of her parents' unhappiness.

Tied with that for the second-worst thing Kate had hidden: that after the single dinner date she'd agreed to, she'd dated Demetri for two weeks, the first two weeks of her third year at McKinsey, largely to make what he'd done to her seem more voluntary, as if she'd chosen it, as if she'd do it again.

And then there was the worst secret of all.

"I'm going to take the condom off now," Demetri said.

Kate said no, but Demetri either didn't hear her or ignored her. Either way, she couldn't move, pinned as she was beneath him, her cheek pressed into the mattress and his hands on her forearms, the weight of his hips against her lower back.

He slid the condom off with one hand and was back inside her, now gyrating his hips, as if giving her slightly additional pleasure was compensation for now being raped.

"I'm going to come," he said.

Three weeks later, four days into a missed period, she met a nice man at a McGill alumni mixer and got both herself and him drunk, taking him home with her at two in the afternoon, knowing, even after their brief few hours' acquaintance, that he would make a wonderful father.

ACKNOWLEDGEMENTS

Thanks:

To my beloved, Andrew Harder, for allowing me to run like a cheetah in the Serengeti;

to my agent, Martha Webb, for believing in this book and in the direction I wanted to take it;

to my editor and publisher, Leigh Nash, for all of the time spent, and for lending her brilliant mind, as well as her patience, to this project;

to my copy editor, Emma Skagen, for de-hyphenating my compound nouns, and my proofreader, Stuart Ross, for ensuring my commas conform;

to my brother, Vamsi Suresh, labour lawyer, who helped me get the tenor of the legal letter Roman receives from McGill just right;

to my three readers, Lindsay Edgecombe, Sam Freeman, and Sarah Fulton, for the vote of confidence;

to everyone who helped me verify details, including Reea Galeano, estate lawyer, and Dr. Ann Korkidakis, OB/GYN, as well as Flavia Zaka, Mike Haslett, Andrew Howard, Angela Livingstone, Dr. Nic Chadi, Peter Carpenter, Prof. Martin Papillon, and Laura Dow;

to Daniel Grenier, author and translator, for helping me pick out exactly the right book for Étienne to give Ophélie;

to Dr. Horia Vulpe, best friend and radiation oncologist, for allowing me to use his dream vanity licence plate;

to my dear friend Dr. Larissa Brewer-García, associate professor of Latin American literature at the University of Chicago, for answering my many queries about academia and allowing me to lend her name to a slightly unsavoury character;

to one of my contacts on social media who used *Father of Two, Husband of One* in his bio, which I blatantly stole;

and to the Canada Council for the Arts, for their generous financial support.

PHOTO CREDIT: EVA-MAUDE TC

Bindu Suresh is the author of the novella *26 Knots* (2019). A former journalist, she has written hundreds of articles for various newspapers, including the *Montreal Gazette* and the *Buenos Aires Herald*. She has a degree in literature from Columbia University and a medical degree from McGill University, and works full-time as a pediatrician. She currently lives in Montreal with her husband, her daughter, and her son.

RECYCLED
Paper
FSC® C100212

Printed by Imprimerie Gauvin
Gatineau, Québec